"I Want
All Over Again,

"Impossible."

"Don't say that."

He was kissing her before she realized his intentions; she was responding before she realized her own. If only the pressure of his lips was not so distracting, it would be so much easier . . .

The tip of his tongue found and followed the intricate pattern of her ear as his hands descended.

"This is a new beginning, Joda," he breathed against her lips. "Everything will be right this time."

ANGEL MILAN

is an adventurer. Though she didn't learn to ski until she was thirty-five, she has tried almost everything else. She is not only a licensed pilot, registered X-ray technician, and a former member of the Denver Classic Chorale, but also the mother of four and grandmother of two. *Snow Spirit* is her first Desire.

Dear Reader:

SILHOUETTE DESIRE is an exciting new line of contemporary romances from Silhouette Books. During the past year, many Silhouette readers have written in telling us what other types of stories they'd like to read from Silhouette, and we've kept these comments and suggestions in mind in developing SILHOUETTE DESIRE.

DESIREs feature all of the elements you like to see in a romance, plus a more sensual, provocative story. So if you want to experience all the excitement, passion and joy of falling in love, then SILHOUETTE DESIRE is for you.

I hope you enjoy this book and all the wonderful stories to come from SILHOUETTE DESIRE. I'd appreciate any thoughts you'd like to share with us on new SILHOUETTE DESIRE, and I invite you to write to us at the address below:

Karen Solem
Editor-in-Chief
Silhouette Books
P.O. Box 769
New York, N.Y. 10019

ANGEL MILAN
Snow Spirit

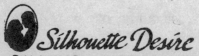
Silhouette Desire

Published by Silhouette Books New York

America's Publisher of Contemporary Romance

Other Silhouette Books by Angel Milan

Autumn Harvest

SILHOUETTE BOOKS, a Simon & Schuster Division of
GULF & WESTERN CORPORATION
1230 Avenue of the Americas, New York, N.Y. 10020

ISBN: 0-671-45161-8

First Silhouette Books printing December, 1982

10 9 8 7 6 5 4 3 2 1

America's Publisher of Contemporary Romance

Printed in the U.S.A.

*Dedicated with much love
to my models of enthusiasm
for the glorious sport of skiing,
my family:
Ted, Terri, Jon, Kim, and Chris*

Snow
Spirit

1

"Look out!"

"Hey! Watch it!"

"Lean on yourself, buddy!"

Joda Kerris watched with amusement as the handsome brown-haired man wheeled and weaved down the slight incline in front of the ski-school sign. One ski on, one ski waving in the air, ski poles under one arm, the beginner was a moving threat to all those around him. They cleared the way for him as he slid on his one ski toward the sign.

"Put your other foot down," Joda called out to him above the squeals of the skiers on either side of the gyrating man.

He tried to plant his skiless boot on the well-packed snow, appeared to be skating for a brief second, then tumbled forward and landed in a heap at Joda's feet. He looked up at her with a grin. Joda couldn't help but smile.

"Sorry about that," he said.

"Don't worry about it," Joda said kindly, and offered a hand to help him to his feet. "We expect a certain amount of 'that' around here." She nodded toward the sign that read SKI SCHOOL as she gave a tug and pulled him uncertainly to his feet.

He had almost recovered his balance as she let go, stood straight up for a heartbeat, then veered forward.

Joda caught him around the middle as his left arm went over her shoulder. She couldn't help but feel the strength in his grasp, and even through her ski glove she was aware of his taut waist.

"I'll get the hang of this. Just give me a minute," he assured her confidently.

He looked down at her as he spoke, his breath warm on her temple. There was definitely a tattletale glint of mischief in the midnight blue of his eyes. Joda felt a little thrill of excitement run through her.

"Can I help you with that ski, Mr. . . . ah . . . ?" Joda reached out to take the ski he still clutched tightly in his right hand before it could decapitate a passerby. The ski was probably two hundred centimeters long, much too long for a beginner. Curious. Joda decided not to say anything about it.

"O'Neill, Egan O'Neill. Call me, Egan," he answered. "Yes, I think I could use some help, thank you."

Joda knelt beside him, put his ski down on the snow, and held both skis still as he pushed his toe into the metal binding.

"Now, push your heel down," she instructed. "That's it." The heel of his ski boot clicked firmly into the back of the binding and Joda reached around his leg to pull the safety straps forward and fasten them around his ankle. "There, that should do it," she said as she stood up beside him. She noted his height as she did so, well over six feet. She felt that electricity again! At five feet, ten inches, Joda was often aware of looking down at the men around her. Egan O'Neill was a delightful change.

"You've been a big help. Thanks again." He planted his ski poles firmly in the snow on either side of himself and appeared to be fairly steady now. He looked uncertainly around.

"Can I help you with anything else?" Joda asked.

"I don't know. I'm looking for a person named Joe—a ski instructor. I'm having a private lesson."

"For beginners?" she asked, teasing, all the while hoping that out of the three "privates" for today, this one was hers.

Egan began to slip sideways, lifted a ski pole, and replanted it. "Would you believe 'intermediate'?" Dimples appeared in each cheek despite his earnest try for a serious look.

"No," Joda answered, smiling, pleased to see evidence of a sense of humor in such an attractive man.

"Fair enough." He shrugged. "Guess you've got me classified. Do you know Joe?"

"I might," she said evasively. "Can you describe him?"

"Oh . . . let's see. The woman said tall, blond . . ."

Joda reached up and pulled the red ski cap from her head. Three feet of cream-yellow hair fell down her back. "Did you say blond?" she asked innocently.

Even on this overcast day without the sun's bright light, Joda's hair glowed with a lustrous sheen. A few snowflakes caught in the silken strands and looked like so many diamonds adorning a flax-golden crown.

"Well . . ." His eyes appreciatively looked her up and down. "What luck. And on my first day out, too. I never would have guessed. Joe . . ." he said thoughtfully.

"It's a common mistake."

11

"I never would have expected . . ."

"A woman to be the head ski instructor." She finished his sentence for him.

"No! No, it's not that at all," he said seriously. "The name just confused me. Is it Joann?"

"It's Joda. Joda Kerris." She offered her hand to him and he reached for it. Even though he had to lift his ski pole to shake hands, he didn't lose his balance. Curious. His grip was firm and sure and he held her hand just a moment longer than was necessary. She knew with certainty that she wanted to experience his touch again.

"Guess you're stuck with me today." He chuckled.

"Don't give it another thought. We'll do just fine. You'll see."

"Yes," he said thoughtfully, "we will."

The low timbre of his voice sent an expectant thrill through her as she began gathering up her hair, giving it an expert twist so that it was easy to tuck back under her knitted ski cap. She noticed Egan was watching her, frowning.

"What's wrong?" she asked.

"I've seen you somewhere before," he said with certainty. "You've been on television. Am I right?"

In the mountains Joda was indeed well known. Her appearances from time to time on the local news programs had brought her an increased popularity in the immediate area. The broadcasts originated in Denver, of course, but few of the big-city viewers shared her neighbors' enthusiasm over her celebrity. She was surprised that this man had seen her and remembered.

"I'm flattered!" she said sincerely, then nodded. "I've done some news spots for Keystone."

"No wonder this place is so popular," he said in soft deep tones.

"Well, thank you." His vibrant masculine voice did strange things to her. She took a look at her watch. "It's just a minute or two until the lessons are supposed to start. Are you ready?"

"Do you always teach beginners?" he asked instead of answering her question.

"Not usually."

"You teach the experts, then?"

She nodded. "Except when I have my handicapped classes. They're my favorite."

"You teach the handicapped classes?" He caught her eye, his interest unmistakable.

"Yes."

"Excellent," he said softly. "We have a common interest."

Joda gave him a questioning look.

"Have you heard of Living Gifts?" he asked.

"A volunteer group in Denver," Joda answered. "They teach handicapped children to sing and paint and do all sorts of things."

"A tremendous organization," he said with pride. "Those kids are great. They learn so fast, they're full of talent. I teach them needlepoint," he added.

Needlepoint! Hardly an established or readily acceptable masculine pastime. Yet he had said it without the slightest apology or self-consciousness. It was rare to meet a man of such courage! Joda looked at him with increasing interest.

"That must be very rewarding. I know my work with them rewards me in so many ways. Seeing even the most minor success is thrilling."

"You're so right." He paused. "It's nice to find

13

someone with similar interests," he said seriously, then grinned. "Your experience may come in handy today."

"Don't sell yourself short, Mr. O'Neill. You look to be in good physical shape to me." Indeed you do! she thought. "I don't think we'll have any major problems."

"I don't think so either, Joda. And call me Egan."

Joda started toward her skis and poles, which were leaning against the backside of the ski-school sign.

"Okay, Egan. Shall we get started, then?" She dropped her skis on the ground and deftly slipped into the bindings, then gracefully bent to adjust a fastening on one of her boots. With the ease of a ballet dancer she moved away and motioned for Egan to follow her. She headed toward Checkerboard Flats at the west boundary of the ski area.

The two-hour morning lesson went well. Joda found Egan easy to work with and very athletically inclined. He caught on to everything quickly—almost too quickly for a novice wearing expert's skis. Curious. Toes in, heels out, he mastered the snowplow and the snowplow turn the first time she showed it to him, gliding effortlessly down the beginner's slope—he was by far the best beginning student she ever had.

At noon, as they walked toward Mountain House at the base of the ski area to have lunch, Joda complimented him. "I think you'll be ready for Schoolmarm this afternoon."

"Schoolmarm?"

"It's our three-mile-long slope for the beginner. You can go from the top down. You'll love it."

"I'm sure I will, Teach." His eyes caught hers.

They left their skis and poles propped against the ski

rack in front of the main Keystone building, entered Mountain House, and went around the corner to the right, into Gassy Thompson's restaurant. Gleaming wood and lush green plants welcomed them into an unusually luxurious setting that was part of Keystone's great charm as a ski resort. Seated next to the mountain-facing south windows, they had a beautiful view of Keystone Mountain and its colorful skier-dotted slopes. The day was still trying to get serious about snowing, but as yet only a few flakes were falling—really a perfect day for early January. And Egan was pleasant company. Maybe more than that. Joda found herself hoping that she would get to know him better.

They warmed their hands around mugs of hot chocolate while they waited for bowls of Gassy Thompson's specialty, a spicy chili that would warm even the coldest of skiers.

"You're an excellent teacher, Joda. Do you like it?"

"I love it. I'm prejudiced, though. I think skiing is the greatest sport ever." Her enthusiasm was showing, as usual. "It offers everything a sport should offer, and it's fun besides." She glanced down at the table, then back at Egan. He was staring at her.

"Your enthusiasm makes you even more beautiful."

She could feel the color rising to her cheeks. His compliments were sincere and very disturbing. She looked out the window and took a deep breath, watching the experts coming off Last Hoot at exhila-rating high speed and careful expertise. Compliments were not unusual for her, but Egan's attention warmed her spirit with expectation. She had liked this unpretentious man from the moment of their first meeting this morning and was disappointed now when

15

he didn't begin to ask her the usual questions one might expect from someone who wanted to get to know her better.

A young man came sliding past the window on short skis. Suddenly he was on the ground, surprised, grinning, unhurt but embarrassed.

Egan watched him for a moment, then turned back to Joda. "I suppose you have a lot of accidents here," he said.

"We have our share. But we have the best ski patrol in the world. They can handle anything, even CPR— cardiopulmonary resuscitation—while transporting an injured skier down an expert slope on a sled. They're quite something!"

"Sounds impossible!"

"I thought so too, until I saw it happen. Incredible."

"I overheard some people talking about an unusual accident while I was in the ticket line this morning."

"At high speeds, a lot of unusual things can happen."

"I guess so. This one was really weird, though. As tight as these rented ski boots are, I don't see how such a thing could happen."

"Oh?" Joda began to feel uneasy, but her memory could not yet tell her why.

"Uh-huh. There was this woman who decided that the rental shop here didn't have a boot that wasn't excruciatingly painful and decided to go over to Keystone Village and buy herself a pair of boots she could bear wearing. At the shop, she asked for the most expensive ones, and at the suggestion of another customer, the salesperson showed her a really fancy pair."

The picture of a beautiful woman formed in Joda's

mind, shining black hair, flashing black eyes, a biting tongue, an insult free with every remark. The steaming chili was brought and set before them. Joda hoped that the interruption would bring an end to Egan's story. It didn't.

"Anyway, she bought the boots and came back to the mountain. But she only got in half a run. Hit a dip in the snow that snagged the tip of her ski, and her foot came right out of that new boot. Amazing!"

"Yes, it is, isn't it?" Joda now remembered the entire episode, but she wasn't about to relate it to a perfect—an almost perfect—stranger. Why was he so interested? Was he frightened? Joda looked at the vitally masculine man seated across from her. No, she was sure fear had nothing to do with his interest, but she added, "I've never heard of it happening before, as a matter of fact."

"You remember it, then, that particular accident?"

His persistence was unnerving. She nodded and hoped he wouldn't question her further, then busied herself with her meal. "Umm, this chili is really good today. Don't you think so?" She looked up. He hadn't taken even one bite.

"Try it," she urged, "it's wonderful." Maybe he would get interested in eating. She hoped so. She did not like telling unpleasant stories about skiing, but if he asked, she couldn't think of a reason not to tell him what had happened.

"You're right. It's great!" He dug in with great enthusiasm; then, after a few bites, he paused, laid his spoon down in the bowl. "How could such a thing happen?" he asked.

Joda searched his fine features for a clue to his interest—anxiety, perhaps—but found only curiosity

17

carved as a vertical mark between elegantly drawn eyebrows. Should she tell him everything that had happened that day? She was beginning to be suspicious of his motives and almost felt as if he were grilling her, but she couldn't find a logical explanation for her feelings—nor a logical reason for not telling him what he obviously wanted to know. Even though she had initially heard it secondhand from the man who worked in the rental shop, she began at the beginning, as she knew it.

"The woman came into the rental shop last week and put Roland through . . . ah . . . a bit of a hassle. Every pair of boots he tried on her just wouldn't do, according to her. They were all too tight. Roland tried to explain to her that the boots had to be tight to support her feet and ankles, but she continued to argue with him about how uncomfortable they all were."

"So she went to buy new ones?"

"After teaching Roland some new ways to insult people that he had never dreamed of, yes. I saw her in the shop at Keystone Village. I had this on." She pointed to her bright red instructor's jacket. "So I guess the woman figured I knew something about ski boots. She asked me which ski boots were the most expensive."

"And you told her which ones cost the most?"

"Yes, I did—Tant Mieux. Someday maybe I'll be able to afford a pair of them," Joda said with a certain amount of longing in her voice.

"So much the better," Egan said.

"I beg your pardon?"

"Tant Mieux means 'so much the better' in French."

"You speak French?"

18

"No."

"How—?"

"What happened then?" Egan interrupted.

"My friend Rick waited on her. He must have brought out a dozen pair of boots. He tried to talk her out of the pair she had insisted on trying—they were too big for her, even fastened on the tightest notch. As I was trying to decide on a pair of gloves, I could hear them arguing. Rick even threatened to refuse to sell them to her at one point. He said he didn't want to take the responsibility for her broken neck. I guess he was trying to frighten her, but it didn't work."

"She bought the boots?"

"She said they were the only ones that were comfortable and wouldn't hear of taking any others. Rick had to bow to her wishes—the customer is always right here at Keystone. He had no other choice, since he'd done his best to dissuade her."

"Did he show her how to put them on and fasten them properly?"

"Of course! That's his job . . . and he's good at it. He not only knows his ski equipment, but he's an expert skier, and a volunteer ski patrol one day every weekend. I'd trust his judgment even before I'd trust my own." Joda began again to eat her lunch; it was almost time to get started on the afternoon lesson. Egan allowed her to finish the delicious chili as he finished his own. He was a good listener, Joda thought, maybe too good.

"Did you see the accident?" he asked as he laid his napkin on the table beside his empty bowl.

Joda wished she could have enjoyed the last of her hot chocolate along with a happier bit of conversation, but Egan was going to persist. Was he always so single-minded and intent? She began again, hoping the story's end would bring an end to his uncommon interest.

"The woman rode Argentine lift up to Jaybird run. I was on my way to Summit House to talk to one of the ski patrol about some new fencing, and she was in the chair ahead of me, riding with a young boy. When they reached the top, she obviously hadn't prepared to get off. She hadn't transferred her ski poles to her outside hand—she hadn't even taken the safety straps off her wrists—and she came flailing off the chair. The boy was almost hit in the head, and I decided that the woman looked like an accident trying to find a place to happen, so I followed her. If she were going around Jaybird to get to Montezuma lift, as I thought she might be, I wanted to ride with her and maybe give her some pointers on getting off a lift chair."

"So did you ride up with her?"

"I never got the chance. She picked up too much speed, couldn't slow down, took off on the road to Erickson lift, and you heard the rest this morning. She fell about twenty yards in front of me. It happened close to a patrol phone—Alice and Patricia were there in less than three minutes."

"That's fast service."

"We're famous for it," Joda said proudly.

"What did you do when it happened?"

Joda looked around the crowded restaurant; there were people waiting for tables. "What say we get back outside before we're attacked for this table?" She picked up her hat, gloves and goggles and stood up to go. Egan silently agreed with her by doing the same. A young couple made a dash for their chairs as they left them.

"Not a moment too soon!" Egan proclaimed, and

put a hand on Joda's waist as they re-entered the bustling lobby.

Joda was on edge. Was it because of his persistent questioning? No. Not now. It was the insistent pressure of his touch. A delicious warmth radiated through her jacket and seemed to touch her heart. He held her tightly, possessively as they threaded their way through the crowded entry, and the masculine fragrance of his cologne unreasonably delighted her. His hand left her waist too soon.

"Well, do I get to try Schoolmarm now, Teach?" he asked as they picked up their skis and poles from the rack.

"Why not? If you think you're ready, then you must be ready. I don't have any objections. Need any help with your skis?"

"I think I can handle them now. Thanks."

She watched as he slipped first one, then the other boot into the bindings. He had learned a lot in just two short hours; he didn't even threaten to fall down this time.

The line at Argentine lift moved quickly and they were soon on their way to the middle of the mountain, seated side by side on the two-person chair lift. Joda's instructions on how to get off the lift were simple and precise and Egan did exactly as he was told. Poles in the outside hand, slide forward in the chair, ski tips up, inside hand on the seat for a push away from the lift, and above all, lean forward! Egan accomplished the maneuver perfectly.

"Congratulations, Mr. O'Neill. You learn very quickly."

"I have the best teacher on the mountain, Ms. Kerris." He bowed formally, his dimples appearing again in a half-smile. His compliments made her heart race in the most unnerving manner. Quite illogical, she told herself as she started right, toward Modest Girl. But Egan turned to the left.

"Is this the run that the accident happened on?" he asked, pointing to the trail sign for Jaybird run.

Joda instantly wished they had taken Peru lift up to Packsaddle Bowl. "Yes, it is."

"How about going this way?" He pointed east.

Joda shrugged. "Okay." She turned around. "Take it slow, though, till you get your 'snow legs,' so to speak."

"Right, Teach."

Joda kept herself exactly even with him all the way to the turn, giving him suggestions on improving this and that. He spotted the ski-patrol phone a short way down the road to Erickson lift and stopped himself in an exaggerated snowplow position.

"That must be the place," he said, pointing down the road.

Doesn't he ever give up? she wondered. Joda was beginning to lose patience. "That's it," she said cautiously.

"Looks flat."

If I didn't know better, I'd think he came here just to hear this story instead of learning to ski. "It almost is."

"Hmm?" He sounded puzzled.

"She was going very fast."

"Looks harmless."

Okay, that does it, she thought. I'm going to finish this tale once and for all; then maybe we can get back to skiing. "Let me show you something." Joda turned almost downhill. "I won't go far; then I'll wait for you. Just watch."

Joda pointed her skis down the mountain, tucked slightly at the waist, and bent her knees. In just a few yards, she was flying. She cut right and edged to an abrupt but perfect stop, then motioned for Egan to come to her. It took him minutes to get to the same position it had taken her seconds to get to.

"Say no more. I think I understand what happened now."

Thank goodness for that! "Shall we go on to Montezuma lift now?" Joda asked.

"Lead the way."

The view from the lift was breathtaking, the mountain peaks that jutted above the tree line glistened with their fresh crystal caps, and a few low clouds could be seen sneaking their way into the valley to the west. Joda and Egan were well above those clouds and the sun peeked out here and there at this higher elevation.

"This is a beautiful place to work," he said, breaking the silence of the ride when they were almost at the top.

"I know. I wouldn't trade it for anything."

Joda expected some sort of response, but Egan remained silent until they were off the lift. Summit House nestled its seven-tiered timbered self at this 11,640-feet elevation, offering its warmth and hospitality to those who were cold and tired. Egan had taken his gloves off during the ride up and his hands were red; he rubbed them together trying to warm them.

"Shall we go inside and warm up before we start down?" Joda asked.

"I'll buy you a glass of wine. How's that?"

"Make it hot cider and you're on."

They sat before the great stone fireplace and sipped mugs of fragrant steaming cider. Both were silent for a time, enjoying the warmth of the fire and the coziness of their surroundings.

Finally Egan spoke. "So, what *did* you do when the accident happened?"

Every muscle in Joda's body tightened, suddenly on guard. Against what? A warning invaded her feeling of ease and she had the distinct impression she never should have begun the story in the first place. "Haven't you heard enough about that accident?" she asked in controlled tones. "I've explained almost everything."

"Humor me," he said insistently. "Tell me the rest of it."

"I thought I had," she said flatly; then, despite her puzzlement and misgivings—and maybe because of his smile—she went on. "I was just passing the patrol phone, like I said before, and I stopped, made the call to the dispatcher here at Summit House, then went to the woman. She recognized me instantly, and the insults and accusations started flying. I hadn't noticed it, but she insisted that something or someone had been obscuring the trail signs. She said she became confused, didn't know which way to go, couldn't concentrate. Then, unbelievably, she began blaming me for everything that had ever gone wrong with her life."

"Were you angry?"

"No. Why should I have been? I didn't even know the woman. She looked vaguely familiar, but then, so many people do, and I had seen her earlier in the store at Keystone Village. I figured she was just a very unhappy person, and her ankle was probably giving her a lot of pain. I tried to reassure her, told her help was on the way. Then I helped the patrol get her into the sled, made sure her skis and new boots got down the hill with her. And that's all there was to it."

"Did you go back and check to see if the trail signs were actually obscured like she'd said?"

Joda was beginning to feel as if she were on trial. This man's power of persuasion was overwhelming and generated from a masculine strength that excited her indescribably. She was powerless not to go on even though some danger seemed to be lurking. "I just had time to get down the mountain to my next class. No, I didn't go back to see, but I found out later that there had been a man in the ski patrol replacing a damaged sign there at about that same time."

"And you haven't heard any more about it since?"

"No. What do you mean?"

Egan paused. "Nothing," he said finally, then changed the subject abruptly. "I'll bet you get asked out a lot, don't you, Joda?" he asked matter-of-factly, as if he already knew the answer.

Joda smiled, glad to be off the subject of the accident. "I do." The danger had passed. She relaxed a bit.

"I don't wonder. You're a very beautiful woman . . . but I guess you hear that all the time. Do you ever accept?"

"Occasionally I accept." She realized suddenly that she wanted very much for him to ask her out.

But he surprised her. "I've really enjoyed my lesson today. I can see that you love your work. That's important to a person's happiness, wouldn't you agree?"

Joda was disappointed and confused that the conversation had not taken the logical next step. She didn't answer his question right away. Had she said something to put him off or anger him? She didn't think so. Maybe he was intimidated by her expertise and thought that she wouldn't be interested in anyone who couldn't share her same skills. No, that wasn't logical either, considering his irrepressible confidence. Maybe he had a girlfriend—or a wife. The thought made her despair. She turned toward him. "Loving one's work is of paramount importance. I do agree. Do you love what you do?"

He hesitated before he spoke. "Sometimes I do . . . sometimes." His voice trailed off quietly and he gazed into the fire.

Joda was puzzled. Almost every man who was a student of hers would finally get around to making some kind of a pass at her, usually asking for a date. Some were older, some younger, some beginners, some experts, some single, some married, and though almost all the offers were rejected with tact and diplomacy, the compliments were not unwelcome. But Egan O'Neill was different. He complimented her in a different way—by telling her what a good teacher she was, how beautiful she was, by listening attentively, by trusting her to be kind with his ineptness at skiing. Most of the men she had ever met would have discarded the idea of taking a lesson from a woman they had met so unceremoniously. She remembered Egan's graceless fall at her feet that morning. Many would have been embarrassed to the point of quitting before they began.

They finished their cider in silence, and Joda had a chance to study Egan's profile as he continued to stare into the roaring fire. He was a well-built man, graceful but solid, with ash-brown hair that was combed straight back away from a wide brow. The beautifully defined jawline was well-proportioned, giving his almost square face a rugged symmetry that accented his masculinity. Joda wished he would touch her again.

She pushed the thought from her mind; it was too unsettling.

"Shall we hit the slopes, as they say in the trade?"

Egan seemed to be deep in thought. "What?" He looked at her. "Oh, sure. I'm sorry. I was enjoying the fire. Okay, let's go. I'm ready." He put his mug down then and stood up. He still seemed preoccupied.

As they approached the doorway, three young girls entered Summit House, talking, giggling, delightfully energetic. To allow room for them to pass by, Joda took a step backward. The full length of her body was pressed against Egan's.

"Thank you," Egan said. He was speaking to the three teenagers.

The girls rolled their eyes and giggled even louder.

Joda glanced over her shoulder and found her eyes caught by Egan's midnight-blue gaze. "Excuse me," she said.

Egan's arm slipped around her waist. "Not for this." His hold tightened; he was no longer preoccupied.

The girls walked on into the lodge and Joda felt as if she should move away, but she really didn't want to. This man had her bewitched, and the feel of his body touching hers was making her indescribably light-headed.

"I think this is the chance I've been waiting for," Egan said quietly, and without releasing her, he went on: "Maybe it's too soon to ask, but . . ." He paused, as if searching for the right words. "I'd like to see you, Joda."

His hesitation seemed to indicate that he'd taken great care not to be too forward. She was touched by his thoughtfulness. Joda felt his arm release her, and she turned toward him.

"May I?" he asked.

"I'd like that, Egan. I thought you'd never ask!"

They began their descent down the west side of the mountain on the beginner's run, Schoolmarm. As Joda promised, it was an easy run. About a third of the way down, they took a sharp right turn to enter Schoolmarm West, and began to make their way back to the other side of the mountain. The going was slow as Egan struggled, but Joda was careful to stay right with him. At about the midway point, she suggested that they take a rest and sit for a while at one of the picnic tables set in the snow-frosted tall pines that lined the slopes.

"How do you do it—ski all day long, I mean?" he asked as they sat down.

"What you're doing right now is the hardest thing you'll do. The snowplow, toes in, heels out, is an unnatural position for the human body."

"I can believe it."

"It's a necessary skill to learn, though. It keeps the beginner slowed down to manageable speeds until he's more in control of his body. But you're well-coordinated, you'll be paralleling before you know it. Then it gets easy. You'll see."

"You mean like that?" He was facing upslope and pointed to a woman coming down the gently graded hill.

Joda turned her head, saw the graceful woman he was undoubtedly referring to. Both skis were in perfect parallel alignment, pointed straight down the fall line as the woman glided effortlessly by them at high speed. She was in perfect control.

"Yes, just like that."

"Looks difficult . . . and easy at the same time."

"It isn't difficult. Trust me."

He gave her a crooked grin spiced with a bit of uncertainty; then his eyes shifted back upslope behind her. In the next instant he had skied from the picnic table and had his arms wrapped firmly around a heavyset woman who was threatening to topple them both headfirst down the hill. But Egan kept the two of them steady as he slid to a turning stop, positioning himself downhill in front of the flailing, breathless woman.

Joda couldn't move. The shock of seeing her raw beginner turn into an obviously experienced expert in a matter of seconds was incomprehensible. For a moment she sat shock-still with her mouth open in surprise. Egan was speaking to her. What was he saying? He was pointing up the hill. Joda turned to look. The woman's ski poles had been left behind her on the slope. They could pose a serious threat to other skiers. Joda finally understood what he was asking her to do.

She stood up and began to sidestep back up the hill to retrieve the ski poles before they could cause an accident. The poles safely in her hand, she turned downhill and skied toward Egan and the woman he had rescued from disaster.

"Are you all right?" she asked as she came along-side her.

"I'm just fine, dear. Thanks to this nice man." She smiled up at Egan and chuckled. "Maybe I'm just too old to learn any new tricks. I was trying a christie turn . . . lost my poles . . . a ski." She looked down at the safety strap still around her ankle and the dangling ski. "Would you believe I've been skiing for ten years and just now got up the nerve to try it?"

Joda wanted to reassure her. "Would you believe I

have a friend who's been skiing for fifteen years and has never tried it?"

"Oh, my, child. That makes me feel much better. I guess some of us are just slow learners."

"And others are very fast," she said through clenched teeth with a sideways glance at Egan.

"What was that, dear?"

"Nothing. Nothing at all." Joda patted the woman on the shoulder. "You're doing just fine. But may I make a suggestion?"

"Of course."

"Keep these safety straps around your wrists from now on. Then you won't lose your ski poles when you fall."

The elderly woman gave her an innocent look. "I don't know what made me forget to do that this time. I always . . . well . . . almost always remember." She shook her head. "You're right, of course. I'll remember from now on."

Joda doubted it, but didn't say so. "Do you think you're ready to go on, or would you like to sit down and rest for a while?"

"Why, I'm not tired at all, dear. And I'm late for lunch. My husband will be wondering what happened to me."

Joda looked at her watch; it was almost two-thirty. The woman saw it too.

"Oh, my!" She took her poles and slipped her hands through the safety loops. "Well . . . he's used to it . . . but I'd better hurry. Thank you both." She turned away and started a laborious snowplow down the hill.

Joda's anger consumed her now. Without a word, she began a sidestep uphill toward the picnic table.

Egan got there just a second after she did. She turned on him. "Just exactly what have you been doing, Mr. O'Neill? And why?" She glared at him.

"I don't blame you for being angry."

"Angry? That's the very *least* of it. Try furious! Try irate! Try indignant! I've wasted almost a full day. And for *what?*"

"I can explain."

"I'm not sure I want to hear it. You'd probably lie anyway, just like you have been all day!"

"No, really, the truth." He held up his right hand as if he was being sworn in before giving testimony. "I'm a lawyer . . ."

"That *woman's* lawyer!" Joda took a deep breath. "Why didn't I think of that?" She put her gloved palms on the edge of the table and leaned across it toward him. "You are very sly, Mr. O'Neill, and rotten, and—"

"I'm sorry, Joda. Really. If I'd known . . ."

"If you'd known what?" she shouted at him. "That I could be so easily taken in? Oh, yes! And then what would you have done? I can just imagine!"

"Joda, please . . ."

"It's Ms. Kerris to you—you . . . you shyster! How dare you come nosing around here, pretending to be something you're obviously not. Well, the inquisition is over. You can be on your way, Mr. O'Neill. Goodbye."

Joda grabbed her poles from the snow and in an instant she was on her way down the slope. She knew instinctively that he was following her, trying to catch up, so she took the left fork at Ballhooter, an intermediate slope, so she could gain more speed. And her expertise paid off. By the time she hit Lower Paymaster, she had lost him, and as soon as she was at the bottom of the mountain she steered straight for the first-aid station at the east end of Mountain House. She had an interesting story to tell the doctor. And a few questions of her own to ask . . . but she couldn't help feeling a sense of loss.

2

Mr. Birmingham, I don't know what else to tell you about the accident. Have you spoken to Dr. White?"

"According to him, the treatment of Shelly Sloan's broken ankle was routine. Everything was done right by the book. It sounds to me like Ms. Sloan's accident was her own fault, but since she was apparently correct about the signs being obscured, she may seek legal advice. According to the doctor, she was blaming you, too, and *did* threaten to sue. It remains to be seen what sort of suit she'll file."

"I suppose her lawyer will advise her on that point," Joda said angrily.

"I doubt the suit will be against you, Joda. There wouldn't be any money in it."

"Does the woman need money? She didn't hesitate to buy the most expensive boots."

"Most suits of this type are filed because of greed, not because the plaintiff needs the money. Shelly Sloan probably has your average avaricious soul. I'm going to call Frank Seagle about this." Mr. Birmingham leaned his six-foot-five frame forward in the chair and reached for the phone on his desk.

"Do you want me to leave?" Joda asked.

Mr. Birmingham shook his head and held up his hand, indicating that Joda should wait. The phone conversation was brief and to the point. Mr. Birmingham hung up the phone. "Frank will be up here this evening, and he wants to talk to you. Are you free for dinner, Joda?"

She nodded.

"He'll meet you at Pug Ryan's Pub in Dillon about seven. Is that okay with you?"

"That's fine. Will you be there?"

"No. I can't make it, but I'll talk to him here before he meets with you. I'm not going to tell him any of the particulars about the accident. I'll let you do that, since you were there."

"I understand, but I have to tell you, I'm really nervous and upset about this whole thing."

"Joda, whatever happens, I don't want you to worry, not about your job or your future here or anything else. You hear?"

"I hear, Mr. Birmingham, but I'm still uneasy. Nothing like this has ever happened to me before. The woman was so . . . well . . . she was so vindictive. I don't exactly understand it."

"There are a lot of unhappy people in this world, Joda. I think it's probably impossible for a happy person to realize what goes on in the head of a truly discontented person. Just don't try to second-guess Shelly Sloan. We'll just relax and wait and see. Okay?"

The phone rang and he answered it, listening for a moment, frowning. "That is out of the question, Ms.

Sloan," he said calmly. He listened again, this time for several moments. "I think you'd better have your attorney contact ours, Ms. Sloan. Have him call Seagle, Ackerman and Rogers . . . yes, that's correct. Good-bye." He hung up the phone and leaned back in his chair, lacing his fingers over his belt buckle.

Joda lifted an eyebrow in question.

"You were right about her vindictiveness, Joda. She wants you fired. Says she won't file suit if we let you go. You heard what I told her."

"Thank you, Mr. Birmingham. I appreciate your support."

"You had no part in it. We'll stand by you."

Joda stood to go. "Thank you again, and I'll see Mr. Seagle tonight."

"Thank you, Joda. See you tomorrow." He waved as she left the office.

The sky was low and leaden now, making the mountain's early evening darker than usual. The gloom was perfect for Joda's dreary mood. She tried to evaluate her feelings about what had happened to her earlier in the day. She had been shaking with anger all the while she had been talking to Dr. White, and the more he told her about Shelly Sloan's outrageous behavior during her time in the first-aid station, the angrier she had gotten.

She felt that Egan O'Neill's misrepresentation of himself was unforgivable. She had heard some outlandish stories about the methods of the legal profession, and now they were confirmed. She had been too young to realize the full impact of the actions of the lawyers and the probate court at the time of her parents' accidental death, but there was almost no money left by the time the courts got through probating their wills. Joda, at age ten, had been taken in by her mother's oldest sister, Hally, who lived in Golden, Colorado.

Highway Six into Dillon was already starting to get icy as Joda drove carefully through the increasing snowfall around the eastern edge of Lake Dillon. The sand trucks were already at work at the major intersections. She passed under Interstate Seventy and took a left turn on Ryan Gulch. Across Windernest to the west, farther up the mountain and into an area where the tall pines had not been cleared away for the purpose of building, was Joda's home, a two-bedroom condominium in the development called Aspenwalk.

Aunt Hally had had the foresight to save the few thousand dollars left to Joda in the wills, salvaged after probate, and Joda had been able to buy in Aspenwalk. It was a beautiful area—unlike those in Dillon and some surrounding developments—tucked and hidden away in the shade and protection of the stately spiked conifers and aspens. Her own home was on the bottom floor of one of the three-story buildings, commanding a spectacular view of the forests from its high-ceilinged wood-beamed living space.

Joda entered the building at the corner, walked diagonally to the center three-story atrium, and looked up. Her pet Boston fern, in one of the suspended planters, was responding beautifully to the extra care she was giving it, and she said "Hi" before she unlocked the door to her condo. After such an upsetting day, her home gave Joda great comfort. Its rustic elegance was a delight to the eye and a soothing balm to the weary spirit, with deep carpeting the shade of soft fallen pine needles that blended perfectly with the rich buff of the heavy oak furniture. The sofa and chairs were covered in a white nubby fabric accented with the warmth of rust and chocolate and peach-colored down pillows. And in every corner and crook, there were green plants, Joda's pride. They grew and flourished while watching the swirling snows of the Rocky Mountain winter blanket the forest floor.

Joda stepped through the glass sliding door at the far end of the living room and picked up a few pieces of firewood from a neat stack in a corner of the balcony-porch, then hurried back inside. She had set up the grate that morning so that it would be ready to start a fire, and she placed the split logs inside the natural-wood-and-brick enclosure and struck a long match to the kindling. It blazed instantly. She sat back on the thick carpeting and watched the fire for a moment. It would be nice to stay at home on an icy night like this instead of having to go out and drive back into Dillon for a meeting with an unknown man about an unknown eventuality, and she didn't feel the least bit hungry. But there was nothing she could do about it now.

A cup of tea was in order. In the small but efficient kitchen at the far end of the living-dining room, Joda put the teakettle on to boil and filled the teapot with hot water to warm it. By the time she was out of the shower, the kettle was whistling softly. The tea-making was a soothing evening ritual which she performed without thinking while she relaxed after a rigorous day on the mountain. After putting the fragrant peppermint tea into the pot, she filled it with boiling water, then went to the fire and gave it a poke, staring as its flames leaped up at being disturbed.

Egan O'Neill had disturbed her in just such a way

this morning. His good looks had attracted her eye, and he had tried so hard to do well in his lesson. His seemingly honest effort had endeared him to her. His work with handicapped children, his unusual hobby, needlepoint, his joy and his candidness had combined with a vital male sensuality and energy that had left her heart beating erratically on too many occasions earlier today. And even now, after his dishonesty had been revealed to her, she couldn't shake the feeling that he was really a man of integrity. But how could he be? She went back to the kitchen, poured a cup of tea, then went into her bedroom to dress for dinner.

Tall black boots, a black alpaca turtleneck sweater, and copper-colored corduroy pants were her choices for the evening, and as she dressed, Egan's smile filled her thoughts. Why couldn't she get him out of her mind? Perhaps she had spent too much time during the day wondering how she might get to know him better. If she hadn't been so distracted, she might have realized what he was doing soon enough to avoid involving her heart. Even more puzzling, he seemed to be as intrigued with her as she was with him. She felt a certain tightness in her chest as her heartbeat began to speed. Just forget it, she told herself. He's a scoundrel . . . isn't he?

Joda hurried to bank the fire; she probably shouldn't have started it in the first place, since she was at home for such a short time, but it was habit, one she delighted in each evening, a joy that ought to be shared. . . .

Pug Ryan's Pub was crowded, busy even on this Monday night. During the ski season it was always this way, Monday or not. The front quarter of the building was devoted to a warm and friendly bar, and as soon as Joda walked in, her attention was immediately attracted to a huge bearded man who, because of his great height and sturdy build, stood out in the crowded room. Before she had time to wonder who he was, he started toward her, his hand lifted in greeting.

"Joda Kerris!" He shook her hand enthusiastically. "Bill Birmingham described you to me, but he didn't come anywhere near doing you justice." His smile was as friendly as his voice. "I'm Frank Seagle. Come on in, I have a table waiting for us." He signaled a waiter, and steering her with a hand at her waist, he guided her to a table next to the windows.

"So, you're Joda Kerris," he said as they sat down. "Makes me wish I was interested in skiing. Maybe I'll just have to get interested!" His rosy cheeks rounded in a smile above his well-trimmed beard. "Wait a minute, I know you from somewhere." He put a finger to his chin, looked up, then pointed at her. "You did that series . . . what was it? 'Ski Tips.' That's it. 'Ski Tips.' Am I right?"

Joda was amazed. Twice in one day someone had remembered her being on television. "You surprise me, Mr. Seagle. Those five spots were only two minutes long, and not being a skier . . ." She looked puzzled. "Well, how did they hold your interest?"

His eyes traveled over her with admiration. "You have to ask?" Then with the twinkle still in his eye, "Sorry. Got carried away!" The waiter was standing silently by. "What will you have to drink, Joda?"

She started to say she'd have nothing at all, but then the thought of the ordeal ahead of her made her change her mind. "White wine would be nice."

"We'll have a bottle of Riesling."

The waiter nodded and left.

"The Riesling here is quite special. I think you'll like it. I hope so," Frank said.

"I'm sure I will, thank you." Joda was pleased with Frank Seagle. He seemed so open and relaxed and happy to be alive. He smiled easily and laughed easily and his gregarious nature was making her feel at ease, as if she'd just met the big brother she'd never had but always wanted. She thought he was probably an excellent lawyer. His large expressive brown eyes were fixed on her. "So, you're Joda Kerris," he said again, this time almost in a whisper. "Tell me about yourself, Joda Kerris."

"There isn't much to tell," she began. But before she realized it, she had told him more than half of her life story, and the waiter had brought their wine and served it. When she looked down, she was surprised to find her glass empty.

"Go on," Frank urged as he poured more wine for both of them.

"So, at sixteen, I started hitchhiking from Golden to the various ski areas around here. I'd go wherever the driver was headed—I didn't care, as long as I got to ski. I guess you could say it became an obsession."

"Didn't your Aunt Hally worry about you? Such a beautiful girl, all by herself out on the road. I'll bet you had some close calls with some pretty unsavory characters, didn't you?"

"Unbelievably, no. I think skiers are, by and large, a basically good group of people, and I never got into a car that wasn't obviously on its way to the slopes. Maybe my good fortune was just dumb luck."

"Luck possibly, but never dumb. I have a feeling you've been very self-sufficient for a long while, haven't you, Joda?"

"I like to think so. I love what I'm doing and I can't think of anything else I'd rather do. Today was the first time I ever experienced any unpleasantry in the line of duty."

The waiter hovered again. "Are you ready to order?"

Frank looked at his watch. "It's eight o'clock! You must be starving." He opened his menu. "Let's see, now, with this wine—we'll have another bottle— something spicy . . . the teriyaki chicken."

Joda nodded her approval as he looked up. She had eaten here many times, and everything they served was delicious. She hadn't thought it possible under the circumstances, but she was ravenously hungry now. Frank Seagle had turned the anticipated ordeal into a party. Amazing! She felt as if she had known him for a long time.

Their waiter was back in just moments with crisp green salads and a loaf of warm and fragrant sour- dough bread. The food was instantly attacked by both of them. Bright lights outside the restaurant windows captured and displayed the crystalline flakes that were now falling in earnest. The bright white jewels against the black velvet of the night sky caught Joda's atten- tion for a moment and then inspired a question. "Why haven't you ever taken up skiing, Frank? You live in Denver, don't you?"

"I guess my hobby takes up too much of my time," he said thoughtfully, "and I think I'm sorry now." He smiled and looked at her with gentle eyes.

"What is your hobby?"

"Don't laugh."

"I promise, I won't."

"Weight lifting. Actually, body building. It's differ- ent."

"Yes, I know."

"You do?" He was obviously surprised.

"I lift weights myself. I've converted my second bedroom into a small gym of sorts. Nothing fancy, you understand, just a bench with a barbell and a couple of dumbbells, but it serves the purpose. Do you train at home or do you go to a fancy gym with all the latest equipment?"

"I'm afraid I've indulged myself to an embarrassing extent. I don't have to leave my home to use all the 'latest equipment,' as you put it. Decadent, wouldn't you say?" He smiled charmingly.

"Enviable, at the very worst." She laughed. "I think people should indulge themselves. I think it would make for a happier world all around, don't you?"

"I've never heard it put exactly that way before, but I see your point. And I have to agree with you. I guess there would be exceptions, though. Some people enjoy being unhappy. Did you ever notice that, Joda?"

"I think Shelly Sloan must be one of those people," Joda said thoughtfully.

The waiter was back then with their second bottle of wine and their dinner. He set it before them, asked if everything was all right, then left them to their meal. They ate with the eagerness of the athletes they were, and with the appreciation due the delicious food that had been served to them, until, at last, both of them were satisfied.

"Dessert?" Frank asked.

Joda leaned back in her chair. "I couldn't," she groaned happily.

"Me either. I'll bet you don't eat many sweet things, do you?"

42

"No, I don't." Joda was proud of her body and the way she took care of it, and it showed.

"And speaking of 'sweet stuff,' why don't you tell me about Shelly Sloan now?" he asked seriously, all business.

Joda began her story all over again, the same one she had told Egan O'Neill earlier that same day. And as she told it, Frank Seagle's reactions and questions were almost the same as Egan's had been. "You remember the accident? . . . How could such a thing have happened? . . . What happened next? . . . Did Rick show her how to use her new boots properly?" And on and on until the end of the story. Joda felt as if she had relived the day just past; it was a tiring experience, and something she never wanted to do again.

"If this goes to court, you realize you'll have to go over all this again, don't you?"

Joda took in a deep breath and let out a long sigh. "I hadn't thought of it, but of course you're right. I was just hoping that this would be the last time."

"I don't blame you. The accident and this incident today were both unpleasant."

"Frank, accidents happen all the time on ski slopes. It really isn't Shelly Sloan's little disaster that's bothering me the most. It was the way her lawyer deceived me. I don't deal with people like that. I'm not used to it, and I don't like it."

"Oh, don't be too hard on him, Joda. He had a job to do and he had to figure out the best way to do it. He couldn't know for sure you'd cooperate. If you had known what he was there for, you probably wouldn't have told him a thing, out of loyalty for Keystone. Isn't that right?"

She nodded her agreement. "You're a kind man, Frank Seagle. I'll bet you don't have an enemy in the world, do you?"

"I have a few. Probably a lot more than I know about. You don't make it in this business without bringing a few people down."

"Well, I'm glad I have you on my side. You're the kind of representative I'd choose if I needed one."

"Would you choose me for a friend too, Joda?" he asked seriously, his kind eyes searching hers for an answer.

"Of course!" she answered quickly, but then she knew that he had meant something more. "You'd be a wonderful friend to have, Frank," she added to clarify her hasty "of course."

"Mr. Seagle?" The waiter was once again at their table, and Joda was glad of the interruption. She'd had enough emotional involvement for one day.

"Yes?" Frank turned to him.

"You have a telephone call, sir. Follow me, please?"

"I'll be right back, Joda. If you decide you want something more, just order it." He touched her hand, got up, and walked away.

Joda sat for a moment looking out into the swirling storm. She felt as if the storm were raging inside her own body. This day had been like no other she could remember. It had started out normally enough—a new student, an enjoyable lesson made more enjoyable by the fact that the student was an attractive and sensitive man who had also found her attractive and interesting. She had felt close to the man, felt an empathy for his supposed embarrassment at being inept, felt a sensual anticipation at his touch. And being so wrong about Egan was a disturbing aspect of

44

the day, too. She had been taken in completely, had not doubted him for any reason or in any way. How could I have been so wrong? she wondered. The revelation that Egan O'Neill was an impostor had been frightening. Am I really that naive? Am I dangerously trusting? Will my "dumb luck" continue to protect me in this deceitful world?

And now it was still "today," and here was Frank Seagle, who could easily be yet another complication in an already complicated series of events. Was he also someone other than he seemed to be? Was he sincere in his efforts toward their friendship, or did he just want to make sure she stayed on the side of the defense? Doubt was a most distressing state!

"Would the lady be comfortable here, sir?" someone was saying.

"Yes, thank you, this will be fine. I'll go get her."

The image of a man standing behind her was vaguely reflected in the glass of the window. He stood with his back to her chair, and she turned and touched the sleeve of his jacket to get his attention. "I'd like a cup of coffee when you come back this way, please," she said to the man she thought was a waiter.

"Excuse me?" He was not the waiter. Joda's heart began to pound. The sight of Egan O'Neill tripped an anxiety reaction she had felt only once before, while hitchhiking. She had not been completely honest with Frank, or with her Aunt Hally, for that matter. Once a man had tried to force her to get into his car. She had been saved from him simply because some friends had seen her beside his sedan and had stopped to say hello. She had run quickly away and literally jumped into her friends' car. They sped away, lost sight of the man, and Joda had never seen him again. How could she equate the two disparate happenings? Was Egan O'Neill such an enemy as that man had been? Or was her heart pounding for a different reason?

Egan recognized her immediately and in an instant he had pulled up a chair and his handsome face was on a level with hers. "Joda!" There was delight and a certain expectancy in his eyes as he looked at her and spoke her name.

She started to push her chair back and get up. Flight seemed immediately necessary, but Egan held her chair firmly in place and wouldn't allow her to leave.

He took her hand. "I have to talk to you, Joda. I have to explain to you—"

Joda jerked her hand away from his and looked at him with fury in her eyes. "That is your problem, Mr. O'Neill. I have no desire to hear anything more you could possibly have to say." What kind of an ego would make him think I would listen to him again after all the lying he did this morning? she wondered.

"I know what you must be thinking about me, Joda. But it's not—"

"You couldn't possibly know what I'm thinking about you. If you did, it would be quite obvious to you that I never want to speak to you again." And as she said it, she knew it wasn't the truth. What was he doing to her?

Egan gave his chair a pull even closer to hers, as if being nearer to her would help him make his point. His knee came in contact with her thigh and his hand once again took hers. She looked away.

"You must listen to me." A finger touched her chin and he gently turned her face toward him. "I'll be back day after tomorrow. I'll meet you at Mountain House as soon as you're off work." His voice was deep, soft and persuasive.

She hesitated. Then: "I won't consider meeting you, Mr. O'Neill, not for any reason." She tried to pull her hand away again, but he was expecting it and wouldn't allow her escape. She could feel the strength in his touch, and it surprised her—until she remembered he wasn't the inept beginner she had thought him to be just this morning. Her imprisonment was illogically exciting.

"I insist, Joda. You have to be there . . . I'll be there waiting for you."

She stared at him with unsmiling eyes, but she knew that the anger was gone from them. She was almost ashamed to admit it to herself—she didn't hate him, wasn't even sure she ever had. Was he feeling her resistance fade? He put his other hand on top of hers; the warmth of it brought a slight flush to her cheeks. She could feel it and hoped he couldn't see it. He seemed so composed. Why can't I be the same way? She usually was calm in all sorts of situations—even dangerous ones—it seemed ridiculous to feel so unsure of herself now. One minute she was angry at him; the next, she was enjoying his touch.

She looked down. Their hands, intertwined, lay in her lap. Joda realized she was enjoying the intimate hold, the surging heat of desire passing between woman and man. It was that same sensation she'd felt as they stood, bodies pressing closely together, when he'd asked to see her again. She was trembling inside as she remembered how happy she'd been because of his invitation.

His hand was gently caressing hers, tracing each finger, generating an unwanted weakness of resolution . . . and a unique weakness of physical strength. Joda fought to understand what was happening to her as Egan's vital presence invaded her senses. She willed

47

her anger to return, but was not completely successful. "I don't want to see you again." She spoke, almost whispering, and knew she had not said the truth, nor conveyed the message of her words. Like and dislike, love and hate—feelings at times so closely related as to be indistinguishable in the trusting heart—clouded Joda's mind with confusion. Could he see it?

"I'll see you Wednesday, Joda." In his mind, the meeting was confirmed. He gave her hand a gentle squeeze, then stood and turned toward the waiter who had brought him to the back of the restaurant.

How can I avoid this meeting? Do I want to? Joda couldn't watch as Egan walked away. Inexplicably, she wanted to be walking beside him, she wanted to feel his hand at her waist, she wanted to experience the caress of his soft deep voice.

Someone was speaking to her. "Joda?"

"What?" Her voice had a faraway sound.

"I said, I'm sorry I was gone so long."

"Oh, yes. That's all right."

"You were a million miles away when I sat down just now."

I was across the room.

"I hope I haven't upset you in any way."

It was Egan who upset me.

"Are you all right, Joda?"

No, I'm not. Joda unconsciously shook her head, then realized what she had done. "I'm fine, really!" she corrected quickly.

"You just shook your head no," he said gently.

"I'm sorry. I must have been thinking about something else."

"The storm is getting much worse. Why don't I follow you home and make sure you get there safely."

"Oh, no. That's okay. I'm used to driving in this

kind of weather, and my car knows the way home all by itself. I'll be fine." She did not want Frank Seagle to come home with her. He might . . . ? Could anyone change her mind about Egan?

"I'd feel a lot better if you'd say yes."

"Really, there's no need . . ." Egan was coming toward their table. Shelly Sloan struggled with her crutches, walking in front of him. Joda's eyes widened with apprehension and Frank turned to see what was causing the interruption in their conversation.

"Well, if it isn't the Irish Wolfhound. Stalking the woods tonight, Mr. O'Neill?" Frank's voice was filled with an animosity that surprised Joda.

"Good evening, Mr. Seagle, Ms. Kerris." Egan didn't offer to introduce Shelly, but proceeded directly to the table beside them. Why couldn't there have been an empty table across the room? He pulled out a chair and positioned it so that Shelly could rest her ankle cast on it when she was seated. He offered her the chair facing away from Frank and Joda.

Shelly waited for Egan to finish, all the while glaring at Joda. She started to speak. "You, my dear, are going to be so—" But Egan put a hand on her shoulder and motioned for her to sit down before she could finish with her threat. She obeyed him without question, but not before a look of disappointment crossed her beautiful face.

As Egan sat down, Joda heard Shelly ask in a hissing tone, "Who is that man?"

And in a voice that Joda could clearly hear, he answered, "In this jurisdiction, Mr. Frank Seagle."

"And elsewhere?" Shelly asked loudly.

"I'd rather not say," Egan answered. "I prefer to avoid a suit for slander."

"We've been rivals for some time," Frank whispered to her; then, to Egan: "So we're to meet again?"

"Your megalomania notwithstanding."

"Delusions of grandeur, eh?" Shelly gave out with a short staccato laugh. It had an evil sound.

Joda was becoming increasingly uncomfortable. Frank Seagle and Egan O'Neill seemed to be bitter enemies. She did not want the venomous bantering to go on.

"Shall we leave now, Frank?" she said quietly, but Shelly heard her.

"Can't take the heat, huh, honey?" Shelly twisted in her chair and gave Joda a triumphant look, but when the brief eye contact ended, she turned back to Egan and found him gazing at Joda, his interest unmistakable. Again she twisted to the table behind her, this time to evaluate a threat. Joda felt the sting of jealous scrutiny even though she was not looking directly at Shelly. "I'll see you at the house," she said to Frank as she stood and lifted her parka from the back of the chair.

Frank looked at her in surprise, but only for an instant. "Yes, of course, I'll follow you." And he did—into the parking lot.

As they stood beside her little white car, Joda tried to explain her subterfuge.

Frank did not want to understand. "You mean you're driving home alone after all?"

Joda nodded.

He seemed confused. "Then why did you . . . ?"

"It's hard to explain . . . I just didn't want the conversation to go on. I don't know what you have against him or what he has against you, and I guess I don't want to know, either. Does that make any sense?"

"Under the circumstances, no. I would have expected you to have more confidence in my abilities in
combat. We are on the same side, after all."

"I . . ."

"It sounded to me as if you wanted to make Egan
O'Neill jealous. Is that a possibility, Joda?"

"That's absurd!"

"Is it?"

3

~eeeeeeeeeee~

It really is absurd! And ridiculous! Why in the world did Frank think I wanted to make Egan O'Neill jealous? Joda wondered to herself as she headed toward Highway Six. He couldn't have been further off the mark! And she had thought Frank Seagle was both perceptive and intuitive! How could he have suggested such a thing?

Evaluating her motives was not one of Joda's strong points; she seldom questioned her own actions, always thinking of herself as a straightforward person with few if any ulterior motives. She was goal-oriented and pursued her objectives with energetic determination without asking herself why. But Frank Seagle's accusation had begun a series of questions.

Had she really just wanted to separate the two men and avoid an unpleasant situation? She could have excused herself and left the premises. For a moment, did she really want Frank to follow her home? If that were so, she had to think of herself as a heartless person because of the way she had discouraged him once they were outside the building. No, she hadn't really meant for Frank to follow her home, but she wasn't really a callous person either. She had to be honest with herself.

Good Lord, I really did want Egan to feel jealous! That was the honest truth of it. And she could hardly believe it.

Joda climbed into bed still wondering what had possessed her at the moment of her subterfuge. What do I feel for Egan O'Neill? She wondered. Would Frank ever forgive her for her atypical, manipulative behavior? Perhaps an apology was in order.

In her dreams, she tried to make amends to Frank Seagle, but every time she met with him in order to apologize, he would transform himself into Egan O'Neill. And at the sight of Egan, her heart would start to race.

How handsome he looked to her; the ever-so-slight graying at the temples lent him a distingué touch, offsetting the disarming smile and intense blue eyes. In her dreams he would reach out to take her hand, and she would awaken in a state of eager anxiety.

Twice, three times, she avoided his touch by opening her eyes and sitting up among the rumpled bedclothes, by straightening and smoothing the sheet and down comforters around her, all the while willing him out of her thoughts and her imagination.

Asleep again, she found all her efforts to dismiss him had been in vain. Her hand was in his now, he was pulling her toward him, and she couldn't resist. Joda sat up with a start, her breath coming in short gasps. She looked at the bedside phone; it was ringing. Of course! Aunt Hally was making her usual Tuesday-morning call, a ritual on Joda's day off.

"Thank you, Aunt Hally," she said softly to herself, then lifted the receiver. "Good morning," she said cheerfully, effectively disguising her disquietude.

"Same to you! I have good news this morning. Kitty is ready to be picked up. The vet called last evening. Nastar has survived his battle scratches and his teeth cleaning and his bath and is wailing for the company of his mistress."

"He probably has the entire clinic in an uproar. I'll come down to Golden as soon as I get organized and dressed."

"I'll see you when you get here. 'Bye till later."

Joda's morning proceeded as usual, yoga stretching, rope skipping, then a session with her weights. There was a difference this morning, though; she couldn't get Egan off her mind, and her concentration was suffering. She was lying on the padded bench, trying to remember what exercise came next, the heavy barbell at arm's length, when the phone rang again. Breathing heavily, she padded into the bedroom to answer it. It was Frank Seagle. He wanted to know if they could have lunch and discuss the possible lawsuit.

"I have to go into Golden to pick my cat up from the vet."

"In Golden, then, okay?"

Joda gave him the address of her Aunt Hally's boutique, hung up the phone and hurried through the rest of her exercises. Trying to compose her apology to Frank now effectively took her mind off Egan. She was grateful . . . almost.

Aunt Hally's boutique was a busy, quaint little slip of a shop on the main downtown street of Golden, Colorado, a suburb of Denver. The place had an Old

West flavor that had intrigued and attracted customers for years, its cluttered interior a paradise for the most discerning shoppers and gift hunters. Aunt Hally had every right to the pride she felt in her successful shopkeeping.

"Want to come back to work, Joda?" she kidded her niece as Joda straightened a shelf full of delicate handmade china-faced dolls. Joda had already told her about the trials she had gone through yesterday.

"Don't tempt me." Joda laughed as she spoke, then changed the subject. "Won't you have lunch with me? You could meet Frank Seagle. He's a nice man, you'd like him."

"I already know Frank Seagle, child. And you're right, he is a very nice man. I'd like to see you two get together, as a matter of fact. From the sound of it, that's entirely possible, don't you think?"

"Not entirely."

"Someone else?"

"Not really."

"Well, then?" Aunt Hally said in her pressuring tone.

The bell attached to the front door tinkled, announcing the arrival of a customer. A well-timed interruption, Joda thought; she wasn't in the mood to discuss her confused thoughts—not yet. The "customer" was Frank. Aunt Hally's tall, slender frame was surrounded by muscular arms in a warm bear hug. She had, indeed, met Frank Seagle before. They seemed to be old and dear friends.

At lunch, Frank confirmed Joda's supposition. Aunt Hally had been a friend of the Seagle family's for almost thirty years. In fact, she and Frank's mother had been Gray Ladies together for four years in the Veterans Administration Hospital in Denver. Until

Frank was eight, he had thought Aunt Hally was really his own flesh-and-blood family. Small world. Small town. Denver really *was* just a great big overgrown small town.

"So, do you have any idea why Shelly Sloan would feel so vindictive toward Keystone in general, and you in particular?"

Frank had told her about a phone call his office had gotten this morning. Shelly Sloan, even against her lawyer's advice, had called Frank to inform him of her intention to file suit against Keystone and to let him know that she intended to try to jeopardize Joda's job position.

"I haven't a clue, Frank."

"Could it be jealousy?" he asked.

"I don't even know the woman. What could she possibly be jealous of?"

"Well, if you two did know each other, that wouldn't be too hard to figure out," he complimented with a twinkle in his eye.

"Thank you."

"But as it stands, jealousy between strangers seems a little farfetched. I guess I was just grasping at straws. Since her case is a bit sketchy, I was hoping to find that Ms. Sloan had some ulterior psychological motive. A grudge, as it were, that she could be talked out of, perhaps. And jealousy accounts for some strange behavior sometimes," he said thoughtfully.

Indeed it does, Joda conceded to herself. "About last night, Frank—I'm sorry for the way I acted. I had no right to use the situation the way I did." Uh-oh! Frank had a suspicious look in his eye. Her apology had followed too closely their discussion of jealousy.

"Are you confessing, Joda?"

"Confessing what?" she asked as innocently as she could.

"That you really did want to make Egan O'Neill jealous by implying I was coming home with you?"

Trapped! She hadn't planned it this way. Should she tell him what she had discovered about herself, what he had perceived long before she had even had the courage to question? *My timing is atrocious!* "Maybe I just wanted to be gone from an uncomfortable situation. I'm not very good at handling them—I'll confess to that." Joda had sidestepped Frank's pointed question, but not too effectively.

"Maybe?" he questioned, his lawyer's instincts showing now. "Aren't you sure, Joda?"

"Maybe Shelly Sloan was making me angry."

"Was she?"

"She might have if we'd stayed longer."

"Why are you afraid of confiding in me, Joda?"

She started to shake her head in protest.

"Are you afraid I'll stand in judgment?" He waited for her answer.

"Maybe," she said quietly, finally.

"People's feelings are their own, Joda. No one is entitled to criticize the feelings of others. How you feel about Egan O'Neill or anyone else is simply your own state of being, not a point of argument." His voice was soothing.

Joda gazed out the east-facing window beside their table. This entire wall of Simm's Landing in Golden overlooked the sprawling city of Denver, but Joda didn't see it. She was looking at the reflection of Frank Seagle's powerful image in the glass.

"And some feelings are better kept private," she said without rancor. Why did she feel that this situation demanded evasiveness rather than her usual straight-forward approach? She couldn't afford to alienate her advocate; still, she was reluctant for him to know the truth of her disturbing dilemma. "I want us to be friends, Frank," she said simply.

"We can be friends, if that's what you want," he said flatly. "And I accept your apology, though it wasn't necessary." He was obviously not totally happy with her reluctance to further their relationship, but Frank was a professional, possessing all the personal security necessary to handle such obstacles. The subject was not mentioned again during their lunch-time together. For that Joda was thankful.

Nastar was ecstatic to see his mistress, and clung to her as she carried him to the car. He honored her with tender ear-nipping cat kisses and loud satisfied purring, and she knew she had been forgiven for what the pale gray Persian must have thought, at first, was desertion. Joda was happy about that; Nastar usually pouted for two or three days after a visit to the veterinarian, and during his sulking, Joda tended to feel lonely. Nastar was good company when he felt contented.

At home, Joda watched as Nastar conducted a thorough investigation of the entire premises, making sure his fifteen-pound body would still fit every familiar crevice and passageway, sniffing everything—he considered it all his personal property—to make sure no intruders had tried to usurp his kingdom in his absence. When he was satisfied that he still reigned exclusively, he took to his throne, the end of the couch nearest and facing the fireplace, and settled down in benevolent dictatorship. His final proclamation before closing his eyes for a nap was concise and to the point, a single glissando in the key of C minor: "Light the fire."

Joda complied. She was, after all, his most faithful subject. The rest of her afternoon went much the same as any other Tuesday was likely to go. She cleaned the snug little condo thoroughly, did her washing, and watered the profusion of plant life that happily shared their living space. As she worked, she wondered what Frank would find out about Shelly Sloan. Would he actually be able to discover the cause of her wrathful vindictiveness? At bedtime Nastar snuggled closer than ever, demanding that Joda have a good night's sleep. And much to her surprise, she did.

"I don't know why you bothered coming here, Mr. O'Neill. I thought I had made it quite clear that I didn't want to talk to you again under any circumstances." Joda spoke as forcefully as she could in a half-whisper.

It was Wednesday afternoon. Egan had shown up at Keystone just as he had promised. Now they were standing in the middle of the lobby of Mountain House amid a swirl of skiers. Egan was dressed in an elegantly cut navy pin-striped suit, silk tie, and light gray wool overcoat that echoed the distinguished sprinkling of gray at his temples.

Some of the people were watching their exchange with more than casual interest, and Joda felt quite self-conscious. Egan, on the other hand, seemed totally oblivious of the stares and attention they were attracting.

"I said I would be here. I'm a man of my word. You'll find that out, Joda."

"I really don't care to find out anything more about

you, Mr. O'Neill." *That's not true!* "What I've learned already is not to my liking, so the answer remains an emphatic no."

"Do you think you need your counsel present?"

"If we ever talk again, that will certainly be the case," she assured him.

"It isn't the legal matter I want to discuss. I've told you that already." His deep blue eyes were steadily on hers.

Joda was trying hard not to be swayed by the power of his persuasiveness. "We have nothing to discuss," she said flatly.

"Ah, but we do." He took a step closer to her, then put his arm around her waist. "There are things going on between us that have to be talked about. You know that, don't you, Joda?"

I love your touch. "No!"

"You can feel it." He pulled her closer. "I know you can."

"There is nothing going on between us," she said too loudly. She glanced around; more people were beginning to stare. "Can we get out of here?" She glared at him.

"There's nothing I'd like better." His arm stayed about her waist as he propelled her forward through the crowd of people and out into the cold afternoon.

Once outside, Joda made the mistake of continuing on to her car. She should have ended the meeting in front of Mountain House, but she wasn't thinking too clearly. Egan had been right: there were "things" going on between them. She felt confused, at odds with herself and the world. Halfway through the parking lot she had wanted to run away, but now, standing beside her car, she had almost decided that facing the problem and talking it out would be the more intelligent thing to do. She did not relish the confrontation, but anything was better than continuing to live with this anxious discontent. In these circumstances it was better to end this particular relationship before it had a chance to begin. The parking lot was not the best place to conduct a discussion, but it would certainly be better than the "onstage" atmosphere in the lobby of Mountain House. Their attraction aside, she couldn't trust him: she already knew that. *He was only doing his job.* Frank Seagle's words came back to her, confusing her even more.

"Where will it be, Joda?"

"Right here is fine with me."

"Keystone Lodge? I'll be staying there."

"No!" Joda knew everyone there; it was worse than Mountain House, and she certainly didn't want to talk in his hotel room. "Right here," Joda insisted.

"I'm not exactly dressed for it," Egan reminded her.

She hadn't thought of that. "I could . . . we could meet later—"

"Now! I want to talk to you *now.*"

"Impossible, Mr. O'Neill. I've had a busy day. I'm going home for a swim before I do anything else."

"That sounds like a pleasant way to end a hard day. I've had one, too, and I have a suit in my luggage."

"I didn't mean for—"

"That's all right," he interrupted, "but I don't mind—"

"Intruding?" Joda interjected. Egan started to speak. "Never mind," she continued. "Let's get it over with. I can forgo my swim for tonight."

"I wouldn't hear of it. I think it's a wonderful idea. I do the same thing myself when I have the time."

"Oh? Are you a beginner at that, too? I don't ordinarily give swimming lessons." Joda couldn't help herself. "I think we'd better stay right here."

He took her car key from her and opened the door. "I'll follow you home."

"You can follow *me* anywhere!"

Joda and Egan both turned to see who had spoken. A jolly rosy-cheeked face smiled at them from just a few feet away. "I'm sorry," the woman said, laughing. "Just butting in, as usual. Hi, Joda. You ready?"

I was supposed to give her a ride!

"You forgot me! Have something better to do?" she teased, then hurried on. "Silly question! I can see that you did." She gave Egan a wide smile and a wink, and Joda had to smile at Betty's continuous ebullient nature.

"Betty, this is Egan O'Neill. Betty Bateman is also an instructor here at Keystone."

"Very nice to meet you, Mr. O'Neill."

"I'm sure the pleasure will be mine, Betty," Egan said with a smile that thanked her for her unconscious help in ruling out the parking lot as their battleground.

"Can I still have a ride to the tennis courts?" she asked, turning back to Joda.

"No problem, Betty. It's right on the way. I'm sorry I forgot."

"I understand." She glanced at Egan. "Perfectly."

"This is a beautiful setting, Joda. You must love living up here," Egan said as he surveyed his surroundings.

"I do," Joda said flatly. Now that they were inside her home, standing together in the living room, she was sure she had made a mistake bringing him here.

"Look here!" Egan knelt to the floor. "Aren't you

beautiful," he whispered, and began to stroke Nastar's soft gray back.

Nastar responded with loud contented purring, filling the room with euphoric music as he rubbed his long body, from magnificent whiskers to elegantly bushed tail, along the length of Egan's thigh.

"Nastar," Joda responded to Egan's questioning look.

"Of course, named after the skiing races. Very appropriate. He looks like a beautiful cloudy day." Egan turned his attention back to Nastar's demands for attention. He seemed so much at home here, and Nastar's attraction for him was unnerving. The cat usually remained aloof and out of reach when strangers visited.

Joda was uncomfortable with the situation. Egan was probably not being sincere in his efforts to make friends with her pet. Neither his words nor his actions had been trustworthy up to now. Joda felt her anger returning.

"Will you stop trying to endear yourself to me by courting my cat? You probably don't even like cats."

"I love cats," Egan said sincerely as he stood up. "I have one myself. As for wooing Nastar, would you rather I was courting you?"

Joda stayed calm. "Under the circumstances, I don't think that's such a good idea."

"And just what are the circumstances?" He took a step nearer to her.

"In the first place, wouldn't you say you have a conflict of interests here, since you're handling Shelly Sloan's case against the company I work for?" Joda asked.

"I'm not calling it a conflict of interests."

"And why not?"

"My personal life has little to do with my work," he said simply, then took another step closer.

"And your personal life has nothing to do with me, either." Joda was trying desperately to remain rational. "It may have seemed possible at the outset, but as soon as your deception was revealed, it was clear to me that any kind of relationship would be impossible. Surely you felt the same way, if you were truthful with yourself at that moment."

His arms went around her waist. "At that horrible moment, yes, it seemed impossible," he said softly. "*We* seemed impossible."

Joda tried to push him away.

"Wait. Listen to me. I said 'seemed' impossible, because nothing really is—impossible, I mean. I've always told myself that, and I have a lot of successes to prove the validity of the philosophy. I want this to be another."

"So I'm to be just another 'success story,' is that it? Another 'feather in your cap,' so to speak. Are you using me to prove your theory yet again, Mr. O'Neill?"

"No," Egan said quietly.

"Then what is it you are trying to prove? Your ability to persuade? Your attractiveness? Your irresistible charm?" Joda was not comfortable with her uncharacteristic cruelty.

"I wish I didn't deserve that," he whispered. "I want to start over again."

She was disarmed by his sincerity, but tried to fight back. "Impossible," she said weakly.

"Don't say that."

He was kissing her before she realized his intentions. She was responding before she realized her own. *He was only doing his job.* Had she really hoped he would stay just long enough to hear her denouncement, then take his leave? If only his lips were not so distracting, it would be so much easier to remember.

But that was not the case. Egan had pulled off her hat; his hands were touching her hair, then grasping it gently to hold her possessively close. Escape was out of the question.

"This is a new beginning, Joda," he breathed against her lips. "Everything will be right this time."

"I don't see . . ." Involuntarily her body shuddered as Egan's mouth traced from whispering lips to sensitive ear.

"But *I* see it," she felt him say against the delicate skin of her temple. The tip of his tongue found and followed the intricate pattern of her ear as his hands descended to her waist, declaring firmly their right to be there.

Why am I allowing this?

"It has to be this way," Egan murmured as if answering her silent question. "Hold me, Joda."

Her arms still hung loosely at her sides, but his soft command set them in motion. Fragments of some lucid argument searched fruitlessly for their fitting-places in a puzzle so nebulous Joda was unable to form its complete image. The present moment became all-important, refuting the past and negating the future, whatever that might be. The male contours formed the shape of her hands, and it became imperative that she experience him more closely. Her fingers slid beneath his topcoat and jacket and brought a vision, yet unseen, of a trim waist, taut and tapering back, its firm tense muscles sculpturing a glorious flare toward broad shoulders.

He breathed an audible sigh of pleasure.

The timbre of his low voice and the feel of his body beneath her hands manifested themselves in Joda as a shiver of desire. She could not deny it: she also wanted to begin again.

Nastar's interruption began with a vibrating humming question: "When's dinner?" It was enough to alert Joda to the progression of things, returning logic to her thoughts. Her hands reluctantly ended their unplanned excursion of tactile delight and fell to her sides.

"No," was Egan's response.

But Nastar answered him with a louder demand than his own. The King was used to being fed at the moment of Joda's daily arrival home and did not want to be put off any longer. It was a good excuse to end her brief foolishness, Joda thought. She turned away, Egan allowed it, and Joda gave a short, almost apologetic laugh.

"He's a very insistent roommate." She still felt breathless and hurried to busy herself with opening a can of Nastar's favorite food. The familiar task highlighted reality for her. She had just given Egan every reason to believe she had forgiven him and was willing to start over. After what had happened between them in the past two days, her response had been totally illogical—unwise, even impulsive, and not at all like Joda Kerris. *He was only doing his job.* Nastar purred a jolly thank-you as Joda put his bowl on the floor.

"I'll have to borrow a towel," Egan said matter-of-factly as Joda turned back toward him.

"For what?" she asked, then realized he was still planning to go for a swim with her. "Oh . . . yes," she answered her own question.

"You still want to go swimming, don't you?" he asked.

She leaned heavily against the kitchen countertop. "Well . . . I really don't think it would be the wisest thing to do. Whether you've understood me or not, I've said everything I wanted to say." She crossed her arms across her chest to finalize the statement of fact. Fact?

"And you've told me a lot more, too," he added suggestively. "We'll wait until after our swim to hear the verdict."

"But the jury is through deliberating," she said without conviction.

"They've decided in my favor. Come on. We'll discuss that decision later." He grinned. "I'll repeat my summation if you like."

What a smile! "All right," she said. He must be the very devil to best in a courtroom!

Egan was already in the pool, his back to her, when Joda came out of the dressing room. Through two frosty windows directly across from her she could barely see the snow-covered ground and walkways surrounding the three-story clubhouse near her condo. Outside, the stately pines and aspens glistened winter-white and snowflakes were falling, while inside, exotic tropical plants thrived in the warm moist air. But the warmth did not keep Joda from shivering. Was it apprehension? She was proud of her body but had always thought it a bit "top-heavy," not quite the svelte model's form she'd always admired but could never achieve. She hadn't remembered feeling this self-conscious, though, since the age of fourteen. *I'll be in the water before he looks this way.*

But she wasn't. Egan turned just as she stepped up to the curving edge of the pool, and began to swim toward her. Joda managed to slip into the water before he reached the side. The depth was about five feet; without calculating the result, she had chosen the perfect setting. Egan was standing before her, and his eyes told her so.

Her bathing suit was the merest wisp of clinging bright red fabric and the water level where she was standing was such that it gave the fullness of her breasts an extra measure of lavish beauty. Egan's hands were on her trim waist and Joda felt caressed by his look of unadulterated appreciation. She had been appreciated before. Why did it feel so different this time?

"You fit my hands perfectly," he said.

The soft undulations of the warm water heightened her awareness of the living, breathing statuary she had become. She felt like a model in the hands of an artist, at the mercy of a sculptor dedicated to precision and faithful design. As his hands moved down from her waist to perfectly describe the curve of her hips, that feeling became profound. Joda remained exactly where she was; her discomfort and self-consciousness of a moment ago had rapidly disappeared and were replaced by a yearning which she could not ever remember experiencing before. And she knew that by just standing there she was making a dangerous choice. Her eyes met his and she was satisfied with her decision. Emotionally, it was the only possible one.

"You're so lovely to look at and to touch, Joda," Egan whispered.

"Thank you." Her voice sounded amazingly steady, reflecting none of the trembling urgency she felt inside. As her hands touched his waist, a moment of doubt accompanied the action. She could, even now, give a gentle push and deny him. But the uncertainty was fleeting. Her hands ascended, her long fingers delighting in the complexity of masculine design. Joda dismissed the feelings of wantonness that beset her as she responded wholeheartedly to his tightening embrace.

"I'm glad you're not afraid of me anymore." His words drifted past her ear in a soft cloud of sound. "You're not, are you?"

Had she ever really been afraid of him? She answered both his question and her own. "No." His sigh of relief praised her answer as his body relaxed against hers. She was imprisoned between Egan and the side of the pool; the internment was exhilarating— and much less easily managed than the challenge of an expert ski slope. Joda felt a strange weakness begin to invade her limbs as awareness of Egan's intentions became more clear.

His hips pressed into hers, his need becoming a reality begging to be noticed. He kissed her shoulder, then nipped at the thin strap of the bikini top. He was pulling it aside with his teeth. The excitement was almost unbearable.

The sliver of red slid down her arm, and so ephemeral was the cloth that it surrendered to the slight weight of the falling strap. Egan moaned with pleasure at the sight exposed by his handiwork. His head dipped down, his lips leaving a fiery trail from her shoulder to the rosy tip of her naked breast.

"No." The word was a plea this time. But this time, the word did not bring her praise.

"Don't say no." He hugged her tightly to him.

Joda tried to gather her senses. "We . . . we're in a public place."

"You let us in here with a key and locked the door behind us." Still holding her tightly, Egan looked around. "We're alone," he said.

"Probably not for long."

69

"Is it always like this when you come here after work?" Egan asked.

"Ski instructors get off earlier than everybody else, and I'm the only one who lives here. Until the manager gets here, yes, I have the pool to myself, but . . ."

Desire flared in the deep blue of Egan's eyes, and Joda reached for the wayward strap and shakily pulled it up into place.

"We came here for a swim, didn't we?" she asked lightly. Surely he wasn't thinking of making love to her, not here, not now! But she had already demonstrated that he could arouse her. Maybe he thought she was a willing partner no matter what the circumstances. She felt a little ashamed of herself; her response to him had taken her by surprise.

"My head is already swimming," Egan answered.

"That doesn't count," Joda said with a short laugh.

"Who's counting?"

"Maybe you should be. Start at one hundred and go backward. That should straighten your head out." She pushed him playfully- back, getting him just enough off balance to loosen his hold on her. She slipped away from him, ducking under the water and giving a strong push off the side, then surfacing several feet away from him just as he turned around toward the center of the pool.

"So that's it, is it?" He smiled that incredible smile. "You'd rather swim than kiss me."

She smiled back. "You had more than kissing on your mind, Mr. O'Neill."

"And so did you, Miss Kerris." No sooner were the words out of his mouth than he had leaped into a smooth surface dive directly toward her, and before

she could take a step backward, her ankle was in his
strong grasp. A pull, and she was in his arms, both of
them underwater. Then she was being lifted up, and
higher, as high as his arms would reach. He was
pushing her, throwing her back into the water. She felt
like a child. Moments of abandon like this were rare in
an adult's life. I want to hold on to this one, Joda
thought as she sank beneath the warm water.

Maybe the pressures of the past few days were the
reason for her need to escape into the world of play.
Or perhaps it was this man, a man who deeply cared
for those who must suffer in this world dominated by
healthy individuals, someone who would risk his pride
to do a job, who could bravely face his critics and
accusers and either stand firm or ask for another
chance. His determination to right a wrong he perceived to be his own fault and his willingness to admit
that he deserved censure were qualities rarely found.
His courage and sensitivity inspired her as much as his
masculine sensuality thrilled her . . . and his ability to
have fun—what a delightful change from the men she
had been seeing lately. Yes, she thought, perhaps
everything will be right this time.

Joda found her footing and stood up. Egan was
nowhere to be seen, and before she could turn around
to look behind her, she knew where he was. His hands
were sliding up each side of her thighs; then his fingers
were slipping up beneath the edges of her scant bikini
brief. The warmth of the water felt unusually cool in
comparison to the heat that suffused her body as his
exploring fingers melted her resistance into reluctance.

His hands continued their upward journey, easing
forward at her waist, rising higher as he stood, finally
resting just beneath the weight of her breasts. He

stood very still for a moment, looking down over her shoulder at the wet and glistening skin of her bosom, breathing softly in her ear.

"I believe you are the most beautiful sight I've ever seen," he said quietly.

Joda smiled, looked back and up at him, expecting a smile in return. But his smile was gone, his eyes lit with desire. She had almost forgotten her resolve. A quick dive would enable her escape. She bent slightly at the waist, and the taut roundness of her bottom touched him. It was no longer just his expression that was reflecting his hunger for her. Joda began to tremble as Egan gently tightened his hold to prevent her escape and lifted his thumbs to caress her already blossoming nipples. She experienced a moment of ecstasy, and for seconds she forgot where they were.

With a touch of dismay, she remembered, but she knew it would be hours before Randy would be coming to open the clubhouse, and only she had another key. Being alone in this "public place" was not nearly as stressful as Joda had imagined before. It was, in fact, the most exciting place she had ever been, a potent provocation. She felt deliciously apprehensive, with no cause to be.

Egan turned her around, and when she was almost facing him, his arms lifted her so that she was floating on her back before him. One arm was over and around her, a hand supporting the small of her back, his other hand cradling her head as his lips descended to hers. Egan's kiss was a fierce demand now.

Joda's arms encircled his neck, holding him possessively, as if he might try to escape. She felt as if they were stealing precious moments of privacy, moments she wished could be stretched into hours. Egan's deception was duplicity no longer. He really had only been doing his job.

His lips were trailing along her jawline. "How did you get this scar?" he murmured as his moist kisses followed the thin straight line from her ear almost to her chin.

"An overenthusiastic student with an unwieldy ski pole."

"I want to know everything about you." His voice was husky with passion.

"It's a long story."

The slight male roughness of his cheek grazed across the fullness of her breast, pushing aside the thin barrier of her bra. "We'll hear it later, then," he whispered, his words being spoken as his mouth nuzzled the firm pink nipple he had exposed.

This couldn't be reality, this crazy abandon, this obsessive yearning, this outrageous turnabout in attitude. Joda didn't want to examine her behavior; there would be time for that later. And yet she had known from that first meeting that their friendship would come to this, that she had wanted it then . . . as now.

Joda's fingers twined in his hair. The pleasure his lips were bringing was increasing to unbearable heights. She was aching to be closer to him, to feel the full length of him pressing against her. She twisted slightly toward him, rolling in his arms, and with a hand on her hip, he helped her to stand. They were near the side of the pool now; Joda had not been aware of their movement, of the few steps Egan had taken while she floated helplessly in his embrace. She could feel the smooth tiles against her back.

Her hands eased down from his shoulders to roam across his chest. Two fingers followed the pattern of delicate design that descended from the lush hair on his chest, down the center of his flat, well-muscled stomach. She stopped at the line of his brief black bathing suit.

"Don't stop." It was a plea.

She hesitated.

"Don't stop." His dark blue eyes were almost black with passion.

Her hands descended, and he gasped with pleasure as her intimate touch discovered the wonder of his desire.

"We should leave," she said breathlessly, but all she really wanted to do was to please him.

"We can't." His voice was husky, but his hands were sure. His fingers followed the leg-line of her bikini, slipped beneath it.

Her heart was racing, only a trace of rationality remained. She tried to move sideways, but his long legs were between hers, forcing them apart, forcing her to remain where she was. The movement only helped him to pull the soft red material aside and expose her to his questing fingers. She felt as if her body had opened itself to an unknown, but irresistible magic.

"Oh!" Her eyes closed in helpless confusion and desire. "You've got to stop, Egan." There wasn't the least bit of conviction in her words. She pressed her legs against his, trying to move them together, but the tickling feel of the soft thick hair that covered his legs against her smooth ones only heightened her awareness of the desire that quivered between them. "Egan, please, we shouldn't."

"What would you have us do at this point?" he breathed.

Her eyes closed again. "Nothing," she said.

"It's too late for that." He was breathing heavily now, his lips nestling just beneath the sensitive lobe of her ear. "Help me, Joda." His lips turned to hers before she could speak and began to draw, from the sweetness of her mouth, the willingness that had been hiding just beneath the surface of her consciousness.

A great wave of longing overwhelmed her, its fulfillment in her hands, its consummation flaming within her sensitive grasp. She could not refuse him, nor would she have allowed him to refuse her. The heat of their bodies formed a feverish circle of persuasion about them in the velvety water. The tips of her sensitive fingers could feel the tense anticipation of Egan's beautifully muscled body as he waited breathlessly for her to do as he had asked.

It was a simple thing to do—to help him. She twisted gracefully as she was filled with fiery exultation and her body lifted to capture the rarest pleasure she'd ever experienced. He cried out as gentle teeth nipped at his shoulder in an agony of delirious fulfillment. Alone in the vast quiet room, the warm water surrounding and protecting them, they shared their joy with the lush and silent tropical plants.

4

~~~~~~~~~~~~

The stolen moments of ecstasy were like none Joda had experienced before. No man she had ever known could have led her into this scintillating adventure. But she had to admit that it had not been Egan who had done all the leading; together they had fallen over the precipice.

And now, still, she was in a state of bewilderment, its only boundaries the strong arms that held her trembling body. She felt innocent yet wicked, dazzled but discomfited, satisfied . . . and not the least bit remorseful.

"I don't know what to say."

"You don't have to say anything," Egan said gently.

"I feel as if I should apologize."

"I never want you to feel that you have to apologize to me for anything." His voice was soothing.

"I've never—"

"I know," he interrupted. "Don't think this was a mistake, Joda." He released his hold on her and took her face in both his hands. "We both wanted this." His eyes searched hers, a probing gaze that seemed to ask for reassurance, even though his words were filled with certainty.

She felt the gentleness in the long fingers that rested softly on her cheeks and imagined how sensitive and considerate he would be with his "children"—the ones he taught. She could see, in the tenseness of his jaw, the determination to comfort her. She became aware of a keen sense of optimism.

"You're right—no one has made a mistake," she said softly.

He pulled her close again, his arms about her shoulders, enfolding her in the surety of his tenderness.

"I've found something that has existed only in my imagination. I'm not even sure what to call it. The sine qua non, perhaps." His words were quiet with reflection.

And indeed, at that moment, the joy they had shared really did seem to be that "indispensable requirement."

"Shall we dress now?" she asked, pulling away and adjusting her suit.

"You're the boss."

"You were pretty bossy a minute ago," she teased.

"And you weren't, I suppose? Come here."

She went happily into his arms again, returning his kiss gladly, playfully. But his kisses were not exactly playful; his tongue skillfully parted her lips, and she could feel that warm hunger invading her body, dictating her intentions. She pushed him away, but she was smiling.

"Oh no you don't. We're leaving this place." She turned out of his arms. "For yours?" He grinned. "That's even better."

She started walking through the water to the opposite side of the pool. "You'd better start counting, Mr. O'Neill."

He was following her. "Backward from a hundred, you mean?"

She looked back at him and nodded.

"You are an unreasonable woman, Joda Kerris!" He caught up to her and put his arm around her waist.

The door from the office of the clubhouse to the pool area opened and two women dressed in warm-ups and carrying racketball equipment stepped out onto the deck. Joda was not even aware of their presence until one of them called out her name. She leaned away from Egan and waved to them. A feeling of normalcy tinged with promise crept through her. But would anything ever be normal again? she wondered. Would Egan change her life?

Joda put both hands on the edge of the pool and gracefully lifted herself out of the water. She made the move look as effortless as a walk up a shallow stair. When she turned around, Egan's eyes were filled with appreciation.

He pulled himself up beside her. "Three minutes," he suggested.

"Four," she countered.

"You're on."

Three minutes had been enough for her. Was it anticipation? The thought of the rest of the evening with Egan, sitting before a blazing fire . . . She was waiting when he exited his dressing room, attired once again in the business suit and topcoat, looking very much the conservative lawyer and very much out-of-place. They crossed to the doorway and stepped out into the silent evening. The snow was still falling, a little more heavily than before.

"Be careful," Joda reminded him as they went up the path to her building at the northern edge of the complex. "Those shoes of yours are dangerous up here in the mountains."

"Don't worry, I'll . . . Whoa!" Egan's right foot slid sideways into Joda's sturdy boot.

Joda caught his hand and steadied him.

"Maybe I need walking lessons, too!" he said with a laugh.

Joda gave him a sidelong glance. "You mean like you needed skiing lessons?" she asked in a playfully suspicious tone. Then, turning toward him and straightening the crooked collar of his coat, "You look as if you ought to be in a courtroom, Mr. O'Neill."

"I guess that's where we may end up," he said, almost reluctantly, as if an unpleasant subject had been interjected against his will.

Was he referring to what had just happened? Surely not. "What do you mean?" They started walking again; she waited three steps for his answer.

"Shelly Sloan wants things her own way," he said flatly.

Joda hadn't thought of Shelly Sloan for hours. Why had he brought the subject up at a time like this? The reality of her life returned in a chilling rush of brutal sobriety. She remembered clearly the moments she had spent in Mr. Birmingham's office while he had spoken on the phone to Ms. Sloan. *She wants you fired.* That's what he had told her after hanging up the receiver. *She wants you fired.*

"Will she get 'her own way'?" Joda asked, fearing the answer he might give.

"Let's not talk about it," he said abruptly.

"You brought it up."

He said nothing. Joda felt as if a door had been slammed shut in her face. "Privileged information?" she asked, knowing what the answer would be.

Egan stepped ahead to open the door to Joda's building. "That describes it pretty well," he said; then he was silent as he followed her through her front door and into the living room. Inside, he stood leaning against the closed door as if debating whether to commit himself to the evening with her or to leave.

Joda pulled off her ski jacket, tossed it on the couch. "I'll start a fire." Then she turned. "Here, let me take your swimsuit. I'll hang it . . . Egan?" He had not moved into the room. She felt impatient. "What's wrong, Egan?" she asked sternly.

He looked troubled and shook his head without speaking.

"Look, I wasn't trying to pry."

"I know. . . ." He handed her the towel he had borrowed, but didn't move away from the doorway. "Joda, lawsuits against ski areas are becoming more prevalent every day . . ."

"I'm aware of that."

"You also probably know that Shelly has a case that will, most likely, stand up in court."

"Thanks to the present judicial attitude, and the treatment of such matters by the press, and . . ." Joda stopped short. She had been about to add, "and lawyers who specialize in extortion." "I . . . ah . . . I . . . just don't understand her belligerence toward me personally," she finished.

Egan turned up the collar of his overcoat. Unbelievably, he was preparing to leave. After what they had just shared, it was inconceivable to Joda that their evening would end so abruptly and on such a decidedly unpleasant note. She began to wonder if what she had believed to be a beautiful and impromptu and inevitable extension of the attraction between two caring adults had really been a preplanned tour de force, an ingenious performance, like his false pose as a beginning skier.

"Just why did you come here tonight, Egan?" Her tone was both suspicious and derogatory.

"Joda—"

"No," she said shortly. "I don't want to hear the answer to that." Another thought was forming in her mind. Preposterous? Maybe.

"Egan, why did you give yourself away to me that first day?" She paused for a second; then: "I'm beginning to think it was intentional." Her tone accused him.

"Intentional?" He frowned.

"My back was to the woman in trouble, but it would have taken you only a second to point to her. You know I could have handled the situation myself."

Egan stared at her, his expression revealing nothing of what he might be thinking, but his hands were clenched into tight fists at his sides. Had she discovered the truth about what had happened at their first meeting? His hand was on the doorknob.

"I'm going to have to leave, Joda."

Angrily she crossed her arms across her chest. "Just like that?"

"I'm sorry."

He didn't sound sorry.

The door closed behind him.

Shocked, she stood still for a moment, her anger growing with each motionless second. By the time she moved to the door, her fury consumed her. She viciously twisted the knob, yanking it open, looked out into the empty hall, then slammed the door shut with all her strength. But that bit of violence was not enough. Joda crossed to the couch and began turning the myriad tiny pillows into missiles aimed at anything, everything and nothing in particular. One soft velvet projectile slammed into her favorite Sanchezia. Bright red stems snapped, lush yellow-veined leaves scattered and fell to the floor. Joda stopped, staring unbelievingly down at the scattered destruction.

A tear rolled unceremoniously down her cheek. She didn't try to stop the flood that followed as she dropped down on her knees and began to clean up the ravages of her temper. Nastar helped in his usual fashion, by getting in the way, rubbing his long length against her wherever he could. His softness and his snuggling were a comfort to her.

"What a mess, huh, Nastar?" she sniffed. "I can't believe I did this." She held up a handfull of leaves for the cat to see. "And all for what? What in the world happened here tonight? Can you tell me?" The clean-up and the talking were drying Joda's tears as she brushed the last of the debris into a neat pile on the hearth.

"Well, I may not know what was troubling him— may never know—but I have a feeling about his being able to separate his private and professional life." Joda backed away from the fireplace and sat on the floor leaning her shoulders against the couch. "I'm not convinced he can do it. Are you?" Nastar only purred. He had no opinions on the matter and wanted only a hug and a comfortable place to lie down.

"Come on." Joda patted her lap. "I'm not mad anymore." Except maybe at myself, she thought. "Maybe I should have kept my mouth shut. Giving himself away . . . it does seem a bit ridiculous. I don't know where the idea came from, it just popped into my head. But why would he ruin a perfect situation? I just don't get it. Do you?'' Nastar kept quiet, the subject was too complicated for him.

"One thing's for sure." Joda took Nastar's face in her hands and looked him directly in the eye. "I refuse to believe he came here tonight to get more information out of me about the accident." Nastar pulled away. "I did think that, you know, when he started talking about Shelly Sloan and what she wants. But after what happened in the pool . . . ? Oh, damn!" Joda hit her fist on the carpet and Nastar opened his eyes wide in surprise. "I just don't understand any of this."

"He seems to be a wonderful man . . . but strange, too. Isn't he?" Nastar looked up at her, his great yellow-orange eyes half-closing in apathy as if to say: you humans analyze a thing to death! Just enjoy and forget.

"I know, I know, you could care less. I understand. I wish I could feel the same way. Maybe I will by the time this mess is all over. But right now . . ." She pushed all negative thoughts out of her mind as best she could, but another tear spilled down her cheek as she stared into the cold blackness of the fireplace.

The snowstorm that had begun on Wednesday night continued for several days. Skiers were delighted, every day brought new powder and new thrills on the slopes. But none of the days or nights brought the call from Egan that Joda was wishing for. Ski lessons were difficult with the beginning skiers. Joda was two instructors short and taking most of the beginner classes herself. By the middle of the next week she was ready for the "Snow Spirit" to put an end to the overabundant gifts; then on Thursday morning she got one of her wishes—clear skies.

Joda considered missing lunch so she could stay out longer in the sunshine, but by noon she was famished. Today, back to teaching the experts, she had skied so aggressively all morning that she just had to have something to eat before the afternoon lessons began. The beautiful weather made the better skiers a little crazy!

But the lovely weather outside did not follow her into Mountain House. There seemed to be a storm brewing in the far corner. She started to investigate the commotion. As she walked toward the administrative offices at the back of the lobby, the glass door slammed open and Shelly Sloan stormed out, rushing by Joda without even seeing her. Bill Birmingham stood in the doorway looking angry. When he saw Joda, he motioned for her to come into his office.

"What was that all about?" Joda asked when she had seated herself in front of his desk.

"Maybe you can tell me, Joda. That woman came in here raving about something between you and her lawyer. She accused you of complicity in trying to undermine her case, and a few other things I hesitate to mention. Do you have any idea what she's talking about?"

Joda's heart was beating wildly, but she kept her composure. "Yes," she said calmly, "I think I do know what she's talking about. Last week Egan came here to see me." She shifted in her chair. "We had a talk . . . We . . ."

"Joda, you don't have to say any more. I can understand what she might think is going on." He ran a hand over the top of his head, closed his eyes for an instant and sighed. "Okay . . . let's see—"

"Mr. Birmingham," Joda interrupted, "why doesn't Ms. Sloan work through her lawyer? Wouldn't that be a more standard procedure than handling things herself?"

Mr. Birmingham's shoulders lifted in a shrug. "I don't know what motivates the woman, Joda. Maybe she doesn't have a lawyer anymore."

"You mean she's fired Egan O'Neill?"

"No, no, I don't know anything like that. It was just a speculation. I don't know anything . . . I don't want to know anything about their end of the case, and Frank Seagle is more than expert in handling matters at this end. I'm going to call him, of course, and he'll probably be getting in touch with you."

Joda stood up to go.

"And, Joda, don't worry about this too much. Seagle will take care of everything, okay?"

But Joda could not get the incident out of her mind all afternoon. By the time she had finished for the day and was changing her boots in the locker room, she knew she was more than ready for a quiet evening at home by the fire.

"They wouldn't fire her, would they?" A woman's voice came from the other side of the room.

"I wouldn't bet on it," another voice intoned. "You wouldn't believe what happened."

Joda started to get up to see who was talking and ask whom they were talking about, but at that moment she heard footsteps coming her way.

"Oh!" Sandy, another instructor there, seemed startled and embarrassed. "Joda! Uh . . . beautiful weather today?" She tried to smile.

85

"Yes . . . it was." Joda didn't try to smile back. Were they talking about her?

"Well, have a nice evening," Sandy said self-consciously.

"You, too." Joda concentrated on tying her boot as she listened to the door open and close. I really don't need this, she thought. Her imagination seemed to be working overtime. I've worked too long and too hard to be head ski instructor to lose it now!

I am the only woman in this position in all of Colorado! Her internal conversation continued as she walked through the parking lot. I will not allow this woman, or anyone else, to jeopardize what I've worked for almost all my life! She got into her car and turned the key in the ignition. The engine turned over sluggishly at first, then tried in earnest to start. I don't need this, either!

"Need some help?" An elderly man standing beside the car next to her had spoken.

"I don't think so," Joda replied.

The man continued to remove his ski boots and replace them with heavy leather shoes while Joda kept up her efforts to get the little white coupé going. Her efforts were in vain.

Joda got out of the car. "The battery seems to be okay. It's new. I can't guess what the problem is. I hate to ask, but would you mind giving me a push?"

"Not at all," the elderly man answered, and in just a few minutes Joda was reluctantly on her way to Golden and the mechanic who had always taken care of the family's auto problems.

If ever there had been a week Joda would choose not to relive, it had to be this one. The weather, the car, the pending case against Keystone, and dominating these at all times, the excruciatingly painful reality of her loss—Egan's rejection. If it was possible to be a "little bit" dead, then that's what she was experiencing. Inside she felt empty, hollow.

Egan's behavior had been baffling, but wasn't her own behavior even more perplexing? In just a few days' time she had come to care for this man—this stranger—more deeply than she had ever cared for anyone else. She had become emotionally involved with him almost from the first moment of their meeting. He had been so unassuming, so easy to get along with and talk to. He had seemed to be a caring person with great compassion, determined to give his time and talents to those who could benefit most from them. And she had given herself to him without a second thought for the safety of her heart. Where is my "dumb luck" now? she wondered. She still wasn't sure exactly what, in the space of those last few minutes together, had happened to change the tender mood between them so abruptly.

I am not an ingenue, she reassured herself. She was well aware of the fact that some people could feel a powerful attraction toward others for a short time, then become completely disenchanted by the revelation of a single fault. But she had always felt that such people were petty and shallow and probably selfish at best. She didn't want to think Egan could ever fit such a description, but the lingering possibility remained.

True, Joda was not a young girl, nor was she inexperienced in love, but being a woman didn't alleviate the pain or simplify understanding; it only made contemplation more rational and less hysterical.

"So you're stuck here. For how long—did Jack have any idea?"

"Jack seemed to think the problem was in the

electrical system. He can get parts tomorrow," Joda explained. "He sends his love to you, Aunt Hally. Said he hadn't seen you for an age."

"Thank goodness," Hally said, and held up both hands with her fingers crossed. "No car trouble. What did Mr. B. say when you called him?"

"He wants me at work tomorrow if possible, but he'll understand if I can't make it. He's calling Frank Seagle; he thinks Frank is coming to Keystone tomorrow and can give me a ride."

"How is it between you two, you and Frank?" Hally asked.

"Same as before."

"Nothing?"

Joda nodded.

"That's a crying shame. You know, I used to think you were a bright girl," her aunt said with a laugh.

"For heaven's sake, Aunt Hally . . ." But she was thinking: I used to think so too.

"Calm down, child! I'm only teasing. I know the chemistry has to be right. If it isn't, it isn't."

Joda turned unseeing eyes toward the beautiful mountain view outside the picture window in Aunt Hally's living room. And even if the "chemistry" is perfect, she thought, there has to be so much more than that! She continued to stare out the window as Aunt Hally went into the kitchen to answer the phone.

"That was Mr. B. Says Randy will feed your cat and Frank will pick you up here in the morning about six-thirty. What shall we fix for dinner?"

"Dinner?" Joda hadn't had any appetite at all since lunchtime. "Let me take a shower first. Maybe I can get more enthusiastic about food after I get cleaned up. Okay?"

"That's fine, dear. Make yourself at home."

It was easy to do that. Joda still claimed her childhood bedroom as her own, keeping clothes and toiletries in her aunt's hillside bungalow for just such times as these. Her shower refreshed her, and by the time she was dressed in navy corduroy pants and a bright red sweater trimmed in navy blue, she was beginning to feel a bit hungry. She had just finished twisting her long hair into a tidy but soft knot at the back of her neck when she heard her aunt's voice.

"The phone's for you, Joda," Aunt Hally called down the hallway.

Joda hadn't heard it ring. "Who is it?"

"I didn't ask. Sounds nice, though."

"Hello?" Joda listened. *No—yes!* It was Egan! He was explaining how he found out, from Randy, the Aspenwalk manager, where she might be, and how it was imperative that they talk. He made it sound like a question of dividend or disaster.

Would he explain what had happened a week ago? He would explain everything, he assured her. Couldn't he do that over the phone? Too impersonal. Joda had to agree that whether the discussion would concern propriety or passion, it should be conducted face to face.

"Half-hour? Yes, I'll be right here." Joda hung up the phone with a trembling hand.

"I take it you have a dinner date?" Hally said with a smile.

"He didn't say anything about dinner," Joda answered in a faraway voice.

"He, who?"

"Oh! I'm sorry. My mind was wandering. His name is Egan O'Neill."

"Do I know him?"

Joda shook her head. *And I don't think I do either.*

Egan's home was situated in the very exclusive area of metropolitan Denver known as Cherry Creek. It was a spacious penthouse on the top floor of a modern twelve-story building, not too far from the Denver Country Club. The furnishings were decidedly "Egan O'Neill," expensive, sophisticated, but inviting and comfortable, with their own appropriateness. In contrast to the quiet elegance, the light gray-blue walls displayed everywhere the many gifts of Egan's handicapped young students. Reflecting talents, skills and energies of every description, the varied and original needlepoint designs also conveyed the love Egan's "children" felt for their teacher.

Joda had had misgivings about coming to Egan's home for their discussion, but now she was glad she had made this decision. The place somehow reinforced her initial, if somewhat intermittent, impression that Egan O'Neill had so many of the wonderful qualities she had felt from the beginning.

Their tour of the artwork on display ended in the dining room on the northwest corner, which overlooked the sparkling city lights of Denver proper. But Joda enjoyed the view for only a moment before being distracted by the most unusual design for needlework she had ever seen. The portraiture was done in many shades of blue, from the deepest indigo to the palest dahlia, and grays, from charcoal to silver-white. A tall, voluptuous woman stood robed in swirling clinging stormclouds in the midst of a midnight sky. Her arms reached out before her, hands together, turned palms down, and from these graceful hands descended a delicate pattern resembling almost triangular but irregular crystalline snowflakes.

"Egan, she's so beautiful! Is this your work?" Joda asked.

He nodded. "The only thing I've done myself in a long time." Smiling, he added, "I was inspired."

"Do you use a model for this kind of work?"

"Not usually."

"Is she Scandinavian?" Joda pointed to the long pale flowing hair, being careful not to touch the delicate work.

"Are you?"

"My mother was Norwegian, and . . ." The impact of what he was implying, that she herself was the model, made her catch her breath. "Egan . . . ?"

He was gazing at her with such intensity she couldn't ask the question, but she didn't have to. He nodded. They stood in silence for a moment.

Joda didn't know what to say; she looked down at the floor. Finally, "I'm honored," she whispered, then looked back into his eyes. "Thank you, Egan."

His arms were around her, pulling her close. "No, Joda, thank you," he said softly into her ear. "I was afraid you'd decide . . . No," he sighed, "I'm not even going to say it."

"Did you do all that work in just a week?" she asked, amazed at the amount of effort he must have put into it.

"I had to. I wanted you near me in some way, in case you didn't—"

Joda interrupted him with a soft kiss. She still wasn't sure where their relationship was going, but right at this moment she cared deeply for the man in her arms . . . and probably always would. They both turned to look at the portrait. "Thank you," Joda said again.

He gave her waist a little squeeze. "Now, you stay right here. I've got to check something in the kitchen. I'll be right back."

Joda took a step nearer so she could see the fine stitching in the lower-right corner. In the silver-white were Egan's initials, but just above it was the name of the work. *Snow Spirit.* Joda frowned in puzzlement. From the moment she had fallen in love with skiing, she had thought of the benevolent forces that brought the adored blanket of winter white as the Snow Spirit. She could not remember telling Egan about the feminine eidolon who inhabited her dreams, nor had she ever heard anyone else use the term. She had been sure that the idea was original with her. A shiver of apprehension made her look away.

Joda turned back toward the windows that looked out over the city. Things were not happening at all as she might have expected them to. No serious conversation was taking place, no explanations had, as yet, been forthcoming. She was completely unable to predict her own behavior from one minute to the next. Perhaps that was because Egan was so unpredictable himself. A many-faceted human being, he had shown her already a kaleidoscope of colorful characters. She felt that she probably would never know him completely.

Until now, Joda had been aware of only two things in the dining room, the window with its lovely view of the city and the portrait which hung on the opposite wall. She glanced about the room. It was furnished as she might have expected—elegantly, in heavy glass, hardwood, and chrome against a background of gray-blue carpeting and walls. The thick rectangular glass top of the dining table caught her attention. It was set for dinner—and it was set for three! *What next?*

As if on cue, Egan came back into the room carrying a round leather-topped stool. He nodded toward one of the chairs at the side of the table. "Will you pull that back for me, Joda?" She did so, and he put the stool down in its place. She must have looked puzzled. "We usually eat in the kitchen," he said with a grin.

We? Is there someone else here?

"Come on, you can help me carry."

Joda followed him obediently into the long shiny white kitchen. A luscious fragrance greeted her and she decided it must be emanating from the two long kabobs lying on a gratelike grill incorporated in the kitchen range. Egan handed her a crystal bowl full of fresh green salad, which she carried into the dining room and placed on the table. When she returned to the kitchen, he was removing the beef and green peppers and onions from the skewers onto a platter.

"I hope you're hungry," he said as he handed her the oval plate full of meat and vegetables.

She took an appreciative whiff of the aroma arising from the food she was holding. "I am now," she said with a smile. "Egan, is this some special occasion?"

"*I* think so."

She decided not to pursue the matter, and carried the platter into the dining room instead. She'd wait and see.

Egan followed her this time; in one hand he carried a small bowl with two baked potatoes. He held it up. "Microwave," he said, to explain how they could be cooked so quickly. In the other hand he carried a bottle of red wine in an unglazed pottery wine cooler.

"I'll get the butter," he said as he hurried back out of the room.

Joda heard a strange sound coming from the kitchen, a high-pitched intermittent whistle. In seconds Egan was back, this time accompanied by an astoundingly beautiful blue Persian cat with large round coppery-red eyes.

"Coventry. Covey, for short," he said, continuing at her inquiring look. "'True as Coventry blue' is an old saying, referring to a blue cloth and blue thread made at Coventry."

"He's absolutely gorgeous, Egan." She was delighted he had been telling the truth about being a cat lover.

Covey wasted no time in jumping up on his stool. He was ready to share dinner with his master, but he sat down immediately and waited politely until he was served.

"You can make friends after dinner," Egan said as he pulled out Joda's chair, helped her to be seated, then took his place at the head of the table. Covey watched patiently as Joda was served, as Egan served himself, as Egan cut one succulent chunk of beef into tiny pieces and transferred them to the plate in front of watchful copper eyes.

"Covey and I get along just fine, as long as I follow orders."

"I know what you mean. You met Nastar. He rules the roost!"

"Would you say we spoil them?" he asked in mock seriousness.

"Let's be kind to ourselves and just say we're a little indulgent."

"A little indulgent." He grinned. "That sounds perfectly acceptable, doesn't it?"

The conversation remained light through the rest of the meal. Egan's culinary efforts had surprised Joda. Somehow she had gotten the impression that he was a man who probably took most of his meals in the finer restaurants about town. Another intriguing facet of his character, she thought as they settled themselves in the dimly lit living room in front of the fireplace. Egan was starting a small fire, and Coventry was curling himself on the gray velvet couch next to Joda's leg. When Egan had gotten the flames started, he turned and sat on the raised hearth facing her.

"I'm no longer on the case," he said abruptly.

Joda sat forward. "Egan, what happened? Why?"

"What matters is that I have done it. That's the special occasion you were asking about."

The questions started popping into her mind. What were his reasons? How did his decision affect Shelly Sloan? Was Shelly's confrontation with Mr. Birmingham today instigated by his decision? How would this affect Joda's position? These questions and many more kept pushing for attention, but most important of all—why? Egan seemed extremely pleased with his decision. Who did he think would benefit from it?

"How did Ms. Sloan take the news?" Joda asked.

"Very well!" Egan's enthusiasm sounded a bit forced.

Very well? Oh, really? "Did you know that she visited my boss, Mr. Birmingham, today?"

Egan abruptly stood up. "She did?" He took the few steps to the couch and sat down, one knee up on the cushion so that he was facing her. "You're sure it was Shelly?"

What a question! "Very sure." Remembering, Joda was trying hard not to get upset all over again.

"What did she want?"

95

"She accused me of manipulating you. She wasn't very complimentary. My scheme was, supposedly, to undermine her case. She demanded that I be dismissed."

Egan picked Covey up from his comfortable place between them and lowered him gently to the floor, then moved closer to Joda and took her hand in both of his.

"I'm sorry, Joda. Shelly's behavior doesn't surprise me."

He's not surprised? How well does he know her? What did he tell her about last Wednesday night that would infuriate her so? Joda couldn't stop wondering.

"I don't want you to worry. Everything is going to be fine. Will you believe that?" A finger gently nudged her chin, and their eyes met.

Joda was far from being entirely convinced, but something in his eyes and his tone of voice assured her of his sincerity, if not his infallibility in predicting the future. She nodded her assent.

"I shouldn't have left you like I did the other night. I hope you'll forgive me."

"Forgive you for leaving?" Joda asked.

"For being so confused. You really threw me a curve when you asked if I had given away my act on purpose that first day. You intrigued me from the first moment I saw you. We had so much to share, if only what we had could have a chance to flourish. I wanted that very much. I didn't know how much until you asked that crazy question. I had a lot of soul-searching to do because I had to be sure."

"You mean I was right?" Joda was thoroughly surprised.

"I couldn't believe it myself, at first. It seemed a barbarous suggestion. I even thought I was angry at

you for suggesting such unprofessional behavior.
That's why I left so abruptly. I couldn't think. For the
first time I couldn't separate my profession from"—he
cast about for a word—"from my passion." He closed
his eyes, shook his head, as if the word he had chosen
was the wrong one, but then he went on. "You were
standing there looking so beautiful and so irresistible
and so innocent . . ."

After what happened in the pool?

". . . and you were making sense."

Making sense? She wondered at his decision to
leave the lawsuit. Mr. Birmingham had told her the
outrageous amount of money being asked for. Egan
was giving up a great deal. Did *that* make any sense?
she wondered.

His hands were on her shoulders, turning her
toward him, pulling her close. Just now Joda was not
feeling the least bit sensible.

5

All the questions that had arisen only moments before vanished with his first kiss. His lips barely touched hers in tentative invitation—a reminder of the gentle side of his nature. Then strong hands were turning her again, completely around this time. Her back to the fire, she faced him, reclining into his arms, her weight across his long legs. Egan loosened her hair, pulling out the one oversized silver hairpin that had held it in place. He drew the golden silk strands over one shoulder, the light color in stark contrast to the red of her sweater, then traced the line of it softly over the alluring curve of her breast. The fleeting touch caused a shiver of desire.

"I see now why your eyes seem to sparkle so," he said, and pointed to the silver highlights in her hair. "You have these same little glitters of light radiating there." Then he was tenderly kissing each eyelid, then the tip of her nose, and each cheek in turn.

Joda reached up and touched his face; every curve and angle, artfully lighted by the flickering fire, was precious to her. Perhaps she did only personify the fulfillment of his passions, but she felt precious in his arms. For right now, Egan's passion would be enough. She trembled as his lips trailed soft kisses down the sensitive contour of her neck, and his hand slipped beneath the bottom edge of her sweater to rest possessively on the flat plane of her midriff.

"I didn't think I could ever want you more than I did last week, Joda . . . but I do."

"Egan . . ." This was probably not the right time, but: "Are you giving up too much—?" She would have finished, ". . . for a taste of passion?" but his kiss interrupted her, conveying an almost desperate need to end the words and thoughts that questioned his motivation and the reasoning for his actions.

The hand beneath her sweater moved up to rest under the seductive weight of her breast, and his thumb began a circling quest to find the limits of its blossoming desire. But coaxing was unnecessary and Egan's hum of pleasure told Joda what she already knew—she was reaching out for him. With every tumultuous feminine invitation for possession, her body was blatantly pleading to be fulfilled.

Touching would not satisfy him. Egan pushed the soft wool of her sweater up to expose the object of his quest. "You are so beautiful," he breathed as his searching fingers pulled the scant lace covering of her bra down to reveal the creamy globe of her breast.

Without hesitation, Joda began unbuttoning his shirt. Her hand slipped inside the silky material to touch the sensuous curling hair on his chest. "You're beautiful to me, too," she whispered. Her fingers found a taut nipple and she leaned forward to kiss it. The male breast was as erotic a stimulant to her as hers to him. She could feel the warmth enveloping them both as Egan groaned under the demand of her clinging lips, and beneath her weight, the solid muscles of his thighs tightened. His own message of need grew unself-consciously.

He was helping her out of her sweater, unfastening her bra, then watching with growing fascination the voluptuous movements of her breasts as she shrugged out of the lacy garment that had bound their weight and freedom. His hand was sliding down the zipper of her corduroy pants. "Take these off for me, Joda."

She sat up, turned, then stood before him, pulling the dark navy material over her hips as she did so. She bent forward to complete the task, completely unaware of the effect her movements were having on him. Before she could straighten back to a standing position, Egan's hands reached up to fill themselves with the ripeness that tantalized him.

Joda felt as if her own body were radiating more heat than the dancing flames of the fire that highlighted her sensuous form. She placed her hands on his knees, let them slide up tense thighs, then higher, to the buckle of his belt.

"Yes," he murmured, his voice rough with passion.

Without embarrassment, Joda helped him, then took both his hands and pulled him gently toward her as she knelt down on the plush carpeting before the fireplace.

"I was a fool to leave you that night," he whispered as they lay down together.

"I was sorry to see you go," Joda admitted.

"It was for the best . . ." He hesitated. ". . . for us." His hand slid down her stomach and came to rest possessively on the curve of hip and thigh.

For the best? Joda hadn't thought so at the time; she had felt an emptiness never before experienced.

There had been friendships in her life, some close but impersonal, a few intimate, but none as intensely promising in shared interests . . . or shared passions.

For us? His sacrifice had made it possible. An artist's skillful hands were exploring the inside of her thighs, caressing, arousing beyond reason. What she and Egan had together was essential to her. His leg pushed over and between hers.

"I won't do without you, Joda."

And she had to acknowledge the truth of her own feelings. Now she knew that if he hadn't come to her, she would have surely come to him, no matter what the risk.

"I want to be a part of your life," his lips growled against her ear. He eased his body over hers. "And nothing else matters but this."

They were lost in the wonder of the moment, both totally absorbed in the ecstasy of indivisible obsession. All the questions that had filtered through had fled Joda's mind. There would be no more leaving, no more losing, no more uncertainty.

Joda awoke near midnight warm and cozy under a down quilt, her head on the pillow Egan had brought for her. Egan breathed quietly beside her, on his side facing her, one hand resting lightly on her shoulder. She was careful not to awaken him as she slipped out from under the cover, gathered her clothes, and made her way to the bathroom. She wished she had a car to use for the trip back to Golden so she wouldn't have to disturb Egan's peaceful slumbers. Perhaps a taxi was the answer, even though he had assured her it was no trouble getting her back to her aunt's house, no matter what the hour.

As she dressed, however, the idea of a taxi seemed

the better solution. There was no need for both of them to miss a good night's sleep. She would awaken him so that she could say good-bye and so that he could get into a proper bed.

When she had finished dressing, she went into the master bedroom, turned down the silky spread and the sheets, then picked up the phone on the bedside table and called for a taxi to pick her up in twenty minutes. While she was on the phone, Coventry jumped up on the bed, surveyed the arrangement of the bedclothes, and gave his approval by settling down in the middle of the king-size pillow Joda had uncovered.

Unbidden, a question arose. Would Covey and Nastar get along? Foolish woman, Joda chided herself. That was not something she should worry about at this point. There were no unwanted commitments on either side. Hadn't Egan made it clear it was only his desire that had impelled him? Not the need for a promise of devotion, certainly not love.

And there was that empty feeling again, just like the one she had felt on the night he had left her. Joda hurried into the living room before she could have time to examine too thoroughly the cause of the nagging discomfort that had invaded the peaceful moment. She had no reason to feel disillusioned. This relationship was entered into without qualms, without misgivings, and with the promise of great joy to be shared by both. She was probably being unfair to Egan, and herself also, by saying that Egan's only attraction to her was sexual. They had many common interests to share and enjoy. Rationality aside, though, the emptiness persisted. There was time, she told herself; she would deal with it later.

Egan was not in the living room when she returned, but by the time she had gotten her coat out of the front closet and retrieved her purse from the table in the foyer, he had come back into the room with two steaming cups of a fragrant spiced tea. He was sitting on the couch in front of the fire.

When she saw him, Joda couldn't help but wonder at his handsomeness. Dressed only in dark gray trousers, his lean muscular body radiated a tense sensuality. It seemed as if the room had been decorated solely as a backdrop for his coloring and good looks, the light grays accentuating the silver in his hair, the blues intensifying the deep blue of his eyes.

"Well, aren't you the efficient one? All dressed and ready to go." He chuckled. "Have time for a cup of tea before we dash off into the night?"

"I have about fifteen minutes," she said as she sat down beside him on the couch.

He looked surprised, but his smile was one of amusement. "Well, that's time enough for tea, and not much else." His arm went around her shoulder. "I think you're going to have to readjust your schedule, don't you?" He pulled her closer and began a trail of soft kisses along her cheek.

Joda couldn't help but smile at her own reaction to his touch. Her need for him astounded her; it was as consuming and powerful as his seemed to be for her. She looked at him, kissed him lightly on the lips, then reached for her teacup on the table at the end of the couch.

"I couldn't see any reason for you to miss a good night's sleep too," she said. "I phoned for a taxi." She took a sip from the cup she held in her hands, then raised her eyes to his. His smile had vanished. "Don't

103

tell me you wanted to go out into a cold night like this," she teased, unable to understand his sudden change of mood.

"I thought we should have a talk," he said in all seriousness.

"Egan," she crooned suspiciously, "you didn't hint at talking when you said I'd have to revise my schedule." She was trying to bring back the playful mood of a moment ago, and she expected him to break into a smile and confess his real intentions. His expression didn't change.

"Joda . . . I want you to quit your job"—his tone was solemn—"before Mr. Birmingham realizes he has to fire you."

"You've got to be joking!"

"I'm not."

Joda stood up, then turned on him. "There's no way that will ever happen, Egan. I am the only woman in Colorado who holds the position of head ski instructor, and I've worked too long and too hard to get there just to give it up. How could you even suggest such a thing as giving it up?"

"Joda, listen—"

"And for what?" she continued, as if he hadn't spoken. "For some neurotic woman's idea of fun? For some lawyer's idea of easy money? I'll bet Shelly's case against Keystone is still being handled in your own firm. Am I right?"

"Joda, sit down here and listen to me."

"So it's true," she said calmly, but her anger was building. "I think you'd deny it otherwise." As Joda replaced her teacup on the table, Egan stood up and caught her hand.

"You're upset. That's understandable." He held her

still, his hands on her shoulders now. "But you have to realize what can happen if Keystone turns on you because of the money involved in Shelly's suit."

"They won't," Joda said defiantly.

"You've become a pawn, Joda."

"Well, isn't that just grand! Or is it a thousand times grand? Is it money that gets 'Ms. Lawsuit' what she wants?"

"You're not being fair, Joda."

"Oh, boy! That's a good one. On me!" She jerked away from him. "Well, I can't afford you, Mr. O'Neill." She reached for her coat. As she put it on, she couldn't resist one last attack of questions.

"Isn't the money enough? What kind of a sadistic witch is this Ms. Shelly Sloan, anyway?"

"Joda . . ."

"Now that you're off the case, maybe you could tell me why she's out to hang me. Or is that privileged information too?" She finished buttoning the navy-blue peacoat and reached for her purse.

"You *do* know why, don't you?" she said accusingly.

He shook his head, but she was almost sure that it wasn't a negative answer to her question; it seemed to be exasperation.

"And you're not telling." She hesitated. "Maybe you're not getting off the case after all." Her voice became quiet. "You're still on her side. Of course. . . . Why didn't I . . . ?"

Her voice trailed off into the quiet of the room. Egan didn't speak. He had either decided she was beyond the point of being reasoned with or he had been silenced by her anger and her accusations. She picked up her purse and hurried to the front door. She knew

Egan was following her, but it didn't matter. Shoeless and shirtless, he wouldn't go any farther than his front door.

As Joda hurried down the hallway, she could hear Egan rummaging through the coat closet. Hangers were falling or being thrown about. "Dammit!" she heard him exclaim as the elevator door opened for her. But his efforts were in vain. As the taxi pulled away from the apartment building, Joda looked back and saw him push open the glass door of the entrance. The building's night guard followed closely behind him; they were talking, Egan gesturing toward the taxi as it rounded the corner.

And there it was again, just like it had happened before, the emptiness, the unanswered questions, the tears.

Is this what it feels like to be a pawn?

"And you believed him?" Frank Seagle was furious, getting angrier by the minute, and the driving conditions on Highway Seventy, with ice and blowing snow, weren't helping to calm him.

"At first I did." Joda hadn't been surprised at Frank's outrage when she told him what had happened last night between her and Egan O'Neill. She couldn't blame him for his anger.

"He's deceived you once already! How could you let him do it again?"

"That's hard to explain, Frank. And I'm still not sure that he has." She hadn't told him everything, of course, and she had no desire to explain how she felt about Egan. At this point in time, she was too confused about it herself.

"You mean you don't feel any doubt?"

"I *did* doubt him. After he told me he wanted me to quit my job, I accused him of still being on Shelly's side and still being on the case."

"And he denied it, right?"

"No, he didn't."

Frank glanced in her direction. "Now, that surprises me." His tone of voice was softer; he seemed a bit calmer now.

"Why does that surprise you?"

"Maybe he is telling the truth, after all," Frank said thoughtfully.

"You're not making any sense, Frank."

"Maybe I'm not." He shrugged. "But this case is a curious one. I've found out a few interesting things this week."

"Like what?" Joda turned toward him, intent. Maybe something would start making sense.

"Shelly Sloan's parents died in some sort of an accident about seven years ago. They were vacationing in Switzerland at the time. Shelly was twenty-four and had been teaching dancing for three years. Making something of a name for herself, too. . . . But her brother was only fifteen, and Shelly took it upon herself to become the parents he'd lost."

"Did she quit her job to do that?"

"Right. Not that they didn't have plenty of money, you understand. Banking. She could afford to keep the housekeeper and the cook and the gardener—and she did keep them, but she apparently thought the boy needed her and . . ."

"Constant supervision?"

"Maybe. And from what I could gather, it wasn't easy for her. Maybe his parents' sudden death affected him badly. He was a rebellious sort of teenager, into everything for a thrill. Shelly's parenting job was a thankless one, besides being nerve-racking, but she was determined to stick it out to the bitter end."

Joda was beginning to see Shelly Sloan in a different light. It was easy to imagine how such a situation could create a lasting resentment, one she hesitated to vent on her younger brother, whom she obviously loved, a resentment she had perhaps decided to direct toward the outside world. Giving up her promising career, Shelly had put seven years of her life into nurturing someone who probably never appreciated her efforts.

"He's twenty-two now," Joda said in a quiet voice.

"Who?"

"Shelly's brother."

"He's dead."

"Oh, no! Oh, Frank, that's awful. After all she sacrificed. When did this happen?"

"About a year and a half ago."

"Was he ill?"

"A skiing accident."

"The poor woman must have been close to going out of her mind."

"According to the person who gave me this information, on the day it happened, Shelly didn't even know where he was. He had a habit of taking off without her permission, not telling her where he was going or when he'd return. She found out from the newspaper the next day."

"Sounds like a parents' horror story, doesn't it?"

"The very worst kind. But it does account for at least some of her strange behavior."

"I agree. I can even sympathize with her now—to some extent, at least. But it still doesn't explain her hostility toward me."

"No, it doesn't. I'm going to keep digging . . . and keep hoping that we'll discover some clue, some point of negotiation, some element we can reason with. There are still too many things I don't understand."

"Like what?"

"Are you ready for this?" Frank gave her a quick sideways glance. "Egan O'Neill was the executor of the parents' estate."

Joda turned slowly in the car seat and began staring out the front window. The snow had begun to let up a bit, but the windshield wipers were still needed. They thudded hypnotically from side to side, the only sound now in the long black Lincoln Continental.

Frank reached over and patted Joda on the hand. "Don't start worrying about it yet, Joda. It may not have any bearing on what's happening today. That was seven years ago."

Seven years ago. Joda, like Shelly, had been at the starting point of her career, but unlike Shelly, Joda had made it to the top. She wondered if she could have been as unselfish as Shelly had been; if she could have given up what she cared for most in her life. Since she had been an only child, she could only wonder.

And where had Egan been seven years ago in terms of his career? He would have been thirty years old, perhaps a struggling and ambitious new partner in the law firm. Could a rich banker's trust in him have been the turning point in his career seven years ago? What did Egan owe to Shelly Sloan and her family?

And what about Frank Seagle? Had his anger at her this morning stemmed entirely from the possibility that she could have jeopardized the case? Or did some of his antagonism emerge from jealousy of Egan O'Neill? They were, after all, professional rivals.

By the time they had reached Keystone, Joda had decided the interrelationships involved in this and probably every other litigation were too complicated to even think about without becoming bogged down in questions, convolutions of thought, and the muddy traps of the emotional past. For the first time since she had begun thinking logically about the law, Joda could understand the need for lawyers' intervening cool-headed service as agents and arbiters.

"Thanks for everything this morning, Frank. I really appreciate the ride . . . and all the other things you're doing, too."

"Joda, I apologize for getting angry." He held out his hand. "Friends?"

She took his hand in hers and gave it a squeeze. "Friends, definitely."

"Look, I'll be over at the Keystone Lodge for a while this morning. If you need anything, just call. What about your car?"

"Jack said the problem was probably a simple one. It should be fixed by tonight."

"Will you need a ride back down the mountain?"

"Thanks for the offer, but one of my instructors lives in Golden. I can get a ride with him."

"Well, call if you change your mind."

"Right. See you later."

But there had been no need to get a ride into Golden, not on Friday, or Saturday, or even Sunday. Joda had called the mechanic, and he had given her the bad news. Jack had not yet been able to locate the problem. His first educated guess had turned out to be only an indicator of the main problem, yet to be pinpointed.

Joda was not upset about the car. She had had to

rent one before; it was easily done through the hotel in Silverthorne, so she was not without transportation. She was upset about many other things, though, not the least of which were the messages from Egan left for her at Mountain House. They came with certain regularity, each more urgent and demanding.

Joda could not bring herself to pick up the phone and dial his number. She did not trust herself to resist his eloquent persuasiveness. He said she had become a pawn. Whose? His own? If she succumbed to his requests, then she would have to think of herself in those terms, and being manipulated and used for anyone's purposes was not to be endured.

But Joda felt trapped in her own home. She had decided to take her phone off the hook every night, and she was, in effect, exiling herself. By midweek she was feeling like a caged animal. Keystone's sister mountain, Arapahoe Basin, just six miles to the east, beckoned to her Wednesday afternoon when her classes were finished. The precipitous Pallavacini Run, the Rocky Mountains' ultimate challenge, was exactly the distraction she needed.

It began on a ridge near the westerly ski-area boundary, then dropped off to plunge into a perpendicular chute bounded by a pine forest on either side. At this late hour in the day, expert skiers had sculptured a fearsome series of moguls in the talcum-dry packed powder. The run resembled the bottom of a giant white egg carton turned upside down.

Joda's concentration was complete, exhilaration at a high level, as she tried to keep her skis pointed as nearly straight down the fall line as she could. She finished the first mogul field and entered a straightaway, hitting close to fifty miles an hour by the end of it, then began slicing and crisscrossing her way through the next series of moguls. Out of the corner of her eye she could see a tall man, all in black, following her too closely. An evasive turn to the right was calculated to take her several feet away from the path he seemed to be following—but he was out of control. The collision sounded like a startling clap of thunder in her head. Then silence.

"Joda . . . ?"

She could hear her name being spoken by a familiar voice, but she couldn't see the woman who was speaking.

"Joda, it's Cindy. We're going to take you to Summit County Clinic in Dillon. Can you hear me?"

Joda nodded her head. The slight movement was the precursor to a monumental headache. She opened her eyes slowly—even looking from right to left caused the oppressive pain to increase.

"Just relax. You're going to be fine," her fellow instructor assured her.

When she awoke next, Joda was on a stretcher in the hallway of the clinic. She tried moving her head, then opening her eyes. The headache was still there, but much less severe. Dr. White was standing over her. "Hi."

"Hi, Doc."

"A bit dizzy yet?"

"Quite a bit."

"I don't doubt it. You took quite a blow, but the X rays of your head and neck were fine—nothing's broken. You have a mild concussion."

She could vaguely remember the session on the cold hard X-ray table. "The man—is he . . . ?"

"He's better off than you are. In fact, he skied on down and called the ski patrol. Didn't need to, though.

Cindy wasn't far behind you. She's going to stay with you tonight—"

"Oh, that won't be necessary." Joda tried to raise herself up on her elbows. Dr. White quickly put his hand behind her head and gently helped her to lower it back to the thin mattress. "Maybe it *will* be necessary," she said with a slight laugh.

"She'll wake you up several times through the night and see how you feel, shine a light in your eyes to check your pupils, get you to say a few words to see if you're coherent."

"Sounds exciting."

"Like a run down Pallavicini."

"Don't say that!"

Dr. White laughed. "You're going to be fine, Joda. I don't expect any complications. Stay in bed all day tomorrow and you'll probably be able to go back to work by Friday, but I want you to check in here first."

Joda closed her eyes and tried to think. "Let's see, this is . . . Wednesday?" Her eyes flew open.

"Super good! See, you're improving already. A few minutes ago you couldn't even tell me your name."

"Very funny, Doc, but I can't miss tomorrow's—"

He held up his hand. "I don't want to hear it. I'll take care of everything."

Joda knew there was no use arguing with him. Maybe he would change his mind. *I'll be in perfect shape tomorrow morning; he'll see.* But of course, she wasn't. By the time Cindy left for work at six-thirty the next morning, Joda felt as if she had been up all night. It seemed like Cindy had awakened her every fifteen minutes for a look in her eyes, a brief conversation and a short walk around the bedroom. And then there were the two phone calls. She had heard the ringing but didn't know what time they had come. A moment of panic had ensued when she realized she had forgotten to take the phone off the hook, but since Cindy was handling it by taking a message, she decided not to worry about it until morning. She'd rather not explain why she didn't want any calls.

After Cindy had left, Joda looked at the two notes lying on the bedside table. Predictably, one was from Egan O'Neill. The other was from the man with whom she had collided on Pallavicini, an apology for skiing out of control, his best wishes, and thankfulness that she was not seriously injured. Rather than upset her Aunt Hally, she decided not to call her about the accident. There would be plenty of time later to tell her about it. She felt tired, placed the notes back on the table, then took the phone off the hook. It was almost lunchtime before she awoke again.

On Tuesday, when she had been off work, Joda had made a pot of vegetable soup. The way she felt right now, she was glad there was something good to eat in the house without a lot of fixing. While her soup heated, Joda took a warm bath. As she slipped into a cozy full-length robe, she realized she was beginning to feel much better. The bath and the delicious soup had worked their magic, and after lunch, Joda felt well enough to recline on the couch and read rather than go back to bed and sleep.

About two o'clock there was a knock on the door, and Joda opened it to find a delivery boy, his face completely hidden by a profusion of fresh-cut flowers, white chrysanthemums, white roses, and baby's breath, in a tall white vase. When he had left, she opened the card that had been nestled in the center of the arrangement, expecting the gift to be from the man who had caused the accident.

Snow Spirit,
The heart has reason that
reason does not understand.

—Bossuet

It was signed "Egan O'Neill."

Joda went back into the bedroom and looked at
Cindy's message again: "He will call back." She had
no way of knowing whether he had or not, but she
was sure he must have tried. Intellectually, she knew
she could not continue to live the way she had been
for the past week. Sooner or later she was going to
have to face the fact that her life must go on, if not
exactly in the fashion it had before, then as nearly so
as possible. She knew her life would be altered by the
addition of heartache and the loss of naiveté. "The
heart has reason that reason does not understand."

With a deep breath and a sigh, Joda replaced the
receiver on the hook. She stood there a moment
looking down at it, expecting it to ring immediately. It
did not. Unreasonably, she wanted to hear his voice.

The rest of the afternoon she spent reading, tucked
up with a blanket and a happy cat in one corner of the
living-room couch. But Nastar's peacefulness did not
transmit itself to her. A phone call was imminent,
wasn't it? Concentration eluded her, the silence tor-
tured her.

Ring, dammit! I hate being a pawn!

6

~~~~~~~~~~

Joda opened her eyes. She had been napping, and now it was dark outside the glass sliding door to the porch. The room was silent; what had awakened her? Then she heard it, a light tapping on the front door. Her first thought was that Cindy had returned to check on her, and she opened the door expecting to see the robust dark-haired woman standing in the hallway.

Her heart began to race. Egan waited patiently to be invited in. In one hand he held a large flat box which obviously held a giant pizza; the fragrance was heavenly. In the other hand he carried what looked like a bottle of champagne. His eyes went to the dining table, where she had placed his flowers, and a slight smile touched his handsome face.

Joda turned away from the door, pulled the velvety blue robe more closely about her and said almost in a whisper, "Come in, Egan. I'll be with you in a minute."

She went into the bathroom. A splash of cold water was certainly in order. Her hands were trembling slightly as she held them under the icy water from the tap. Joda took her time, trying to gather her thoughts as she brushed her long straight hair and pulled it back on either side with two silver barrettes. The mirror reflected the same person she had seen there yesterday; there wasn't even a bruise to show what she had been through. Neither the accident of yesterday nor the torment of the week was anywhere in evidence. The bruises were inside.

"Joda, are you all right?" Egan's voice came through the closed door.

How long have I been in here? she wondered. "I'm fine." She opened the door to a worried look. "Really, I'm fine." The worried look almost disappeared. *Longer than I thought.*

He rubbed his hands together. "I've started a fire. I hope you don't mind. And I fed Nastar," he said as he put his arm around her shoulder and guided her the few steps into the living room. "Now, I want you to sit down here on the couch and just relax. I'll take care of everything." He helped her to get comfortable, then moved to the dining table, where he had already set out two plates, glasses, forks and napkins.

The fire he had started was already blazing, its warmth and light bringing a cozy and cheerful feeling into the room. The heat felt good. Under the circumstances, Joda did not think she would be able to eat, but after a few bites of the delicious pizza, her inner turmoil could no longer mask her hunger. She picked up the wineglass from the small square table in front of the couch and held it up. "This isn't alcoholic, is it?"

"Of course not! Cindy told me what happened. I knew you couldn't have any alcohol. It's a sparkling apple cider and nothing else. . . . Joda, I'm so glad you're all right."

"You're very thoughtful, Egan," she said quietly,

then took a sip of the refreshing amber liquid and replaced the glass on the table.

"And very stupid sometimes, too. Joda, I may not deserve it, but would you hear me out this time?"

She took the last bite of her pizza, then set her plate on the table. Leaning back on the couch, she closed her eyes for a moment. She had already decided to hear whatever he had to say earlier that afternoon, at the moment when she replaced the phone receiver on the hook. It would be harder, but perhaps it was better that they were face to face. She reached for her glass of cider, then turned toward him, one knee bent up on the cushions. "I'll listen, Egan. But only if you're prepared to talk in light of the fact that I have no intention whatsoever of quitting my job. Agreed?"

A questioning frown clouded his expression, but only for a fleeting second. "Agreed." He put his plate down. "Mainly, I wanted you to understand the reasoning behind my suggestion."

"It was a request, Egan, not a suggestion. In fact, for a moment I thought it sounded a little like an order."

"I'm sorry about that. But I know how you love your work. I was trying to figure all the angles."

"Like what?"

"Like, what if Shelly decides that getting you fired is more important than the money involved?"

"Why would she do that?"

Egan ignored the question and went on with his thought. "She might bargain with the ski area to drop the case in exchange for your dismissal. It would be an attractive offer for Keystone."

"She wouldn't do that!" Joda said unbelievingly.

"Can you say that with complete certainty, Joda?"

She couldn't really fault him for being highly analytical of the situation, and she had to admit, "I'm more confused about this with every day that goes by, Egan. I keep hoping someone will shed some light on the subject. Nothing, except the móney involved, makes any kind of sense to me."

"What makes sense to me is this—if you resign, the likelihood of your getting a job in the same position at another ski area is much better. You're popular and well-known, a real asset to any resort. Think about what you've done for Keystone. On the other hand, if you go looking for a job after being fired from this one, believe me, it will be very difficult for anyone to look favorably at that fact, especially if they're hiring a head ski instructor."

"I guess I'll just have to deal with that when it happens, *if* it happens, and I really don't think it will. I have no connection at all with Shelly Sloan or her life except for our brief meeting on the day of her accident. She has no motive I can think of for the stance she's taken against me. I think the woman will come to her senses finally and change her mind."

"And what makes you think that?"

Joda didn't want to answer the question. She still had no idea what relationship existed between Egan and Shelly. And even if she could find out, she wasn't sure she wanted to know. Frank Seagle had already found out quite a bit about the mysterious Ms. Sloan, and he would in all probability find out still more. If Joda answered Egan's question honestly, she might divulge something Frank had told her in confidence. Joda had just said that she had no idea what might be motivating Shelly, but there was one possibility that Frank's information had suggested. Joda had been successful in her career; Shelly had not. It was implausible, true enough, but the jealousy Frank had asked about before just might be a factor worth considering if one thought about it in a different context. Egan was waiting for an answer to his question.

"I'm not sure." It wasn't a lie.

Egan reached out and took her face in both his hands. "Joda, my gentle naive woman." His thumb outlined her sensitive lips with a caressing touch. "I'm only trying to protect you." He eased himself closer to her, encircling her with protective arms, pulling her nearer to him. "There are people in this world who will care nothing for your tender heart, Joda." His hand was moving up and down her arm as if he were trying to soothe a frightened child. "I'm going to help you with this."

But Joda was not only thinking of her predicament involving the lawsuit. She was also thinking of the confusion concerning how she felt about Egan. Whether she was emotionally ready to deal with it or not, she could feel herself falling in love with him—and she had never used the word "love" to describe her feelings for any man before. She had railed against it, denied it, battled it with all the emotional strength she possessed, but it was useless to fight it any longer.

She had judged him harshly on two occasions, turning away from him in anger and causing both of them pain. And hadn't he been the one who always took the indefensible and psychologically dangerous first step toward understanding and reconciliation—each time chancing another rejection? Even so, Joda was certain that he was not in love with her. He was keeping his distance somehow; there seemed to be a corner of his mind reserved for another part of his life.

At this moment Joda was sure of only one thing—Egan was not in that group of people who cared nothing for her tender heart. Despite all the questions that remained to be answered, Joda was convinced that Egan was concerned with her welfare. He was sincere in his desire to help, but would he be able to? The atmosphere was apprehensive despite the cheerful fire.

"Why don't we just wait and see, Egan. My intuition tells me everything will turn out all right."

"But mine"—he hesitated—"is telling me something else."

His hesitation, yet another indication of that private portion of his life, troubled Joda. She felt certain that Frank would find out about it, and she was almost sure she didn't want to know the secret.

She changed the subject. "The flowers are beautiful. Thank you."

"A peace offering." He smiled. "You've done a pretty good job of ignoring me for the past few days."

"Taking the phone off the hook was one of the more foolish things I've done in my life. Avoiding conflict isn't usually my style." She laughed. "I guess I've never had quite this much at one time, though."

The phone rang. "Will you get that?" she asked.

"Sure. Bedroom?"

She nodded.

His absence from the room made their closeness of a moment ago seem all the more precious. It was almost as if Egan represented something that had been missing from her life up until the time he had entered it. The intensity of the conflict between them had been acute from the very beginning, but somehow, mostly through his efforts, the contentions had been overcome. And each time the hostility had been talked through, their bond had seemed to be all the more consuming, at least for Joda.

Egan was staying overlong in the bedroom, so she decided to investigate.

"Who was it?" she asked as she came into the room.

Egan was busy straightening the bedcovers, his back to her. "Cindy," he said. "She brought your rental car back to Keystone, and somebody named Jack called and told Mr. Birmingham that your car was repaired and ready to be picked up. I think she said it was a problem with the ground strap. Hard to find, but four dollars fixed it. How about that?"

"That's a relief!" Joda was beginning to wonder why he was going on so. "Egan, what time will Cindy be here in the morning?"

"She won't."

"Oh, boy, I'd better call her back and work something out."

"That won't be necessary," he said abruptly, then turned to her. "I told her you already had a ride."

"I don't."

"You do . . . if you want it."

Joda stared at him, the realization dawning that he was proposing to stay the night and drive her himself. And that's exactly what she wanted him to do.

"Yes," she said, "that's fine, Egan."

"Now, I want you to get ready for bed. Don't worry about the kitchen or the dishes or anything. I'll take care of all that. I want you to rest."

Joda started to follow him back into the living room.

"You heard me. Doctor's orders. Rest!"

"Doctor's orders?" She grinned, loving his attention.

"Well, not really. Mine. Now, get a move on!"

Not since she had moved from Aunt Hally's had Joda been treated in this pontifical manner. Could Egan have taken lessons from her? But it was his obvious concern for her health and comfort that warmed her heart. Joda went into the bathroom and brushed her teeth, then shrugged out of her robe and put on the delicate sky-blue teddy that was hanging on the back of the bathroom door. Once back into her robe, she opened the door to find Egan spreading a blanket out on the couch. He must have checked out the linen closet while she was dressing. He had apparently made a trip out to his car too, as a black leather zippered case lay on the floor near the fireplace.

"I'll get you a pillow." And she was back in seconds with one filled with fluffy down.

"Perfect. Thanks."

"Are you sure you're going to be comfortable there? I'm used to it. I can take the couch, and you can take the bed. I don't mind." Funny, how his staying seemed like the most natural thing that could happen.

"Wouldn't hear of it."

"It makes into a bed . . ."

"This is fine. You need your rest, and the best place to get it is in your own bed." They were standing close together, side by side. His arm slipped around her waist, and he drew her closer. "Now, give me a kiss to sleep on and get in there."

Joda gladly wrapped her arms around his neck and kissed him lightly on the lips, then leaned her head slightly back. "Thank you for everything, Egan, and I'm sorry about our misunderstanding." She gave him another gentle kiss.

"You can do better than that," he said as she started to pull away again. His head bent down to hers.

At first his tenderness spoke eloquently of his affection for her, and she was assailed by the hypnotic effect of his touch. She melted against him, responding now without the least apprehension or misgiving about the future. His mouth was opening slightly, as was hers, and she could feel the moist warmth begin to melt away the sensible thoughts of a restful night.

But he was not to be swayed. He lifted his lips from hers. "See, I told you you could do better. Now I want you to get some sleep. Tomorrow may be harder than you think it's going to be. I know about these things." He gave her a quick hug, then turned her around. "Do you want me to tuck you in?" he said with a chuckle.

She glanced back at him. "Unnecessary, Mr. O'Neill."

But after she had gotten into bed and pulled the covers up over herself, she wished she had said yes. His kiss, as brief as it had been, had stirred her to that incredible point of longing again. The physical attraction she felt for him amazed her, but there was something more, too. The addition was not easy to pinpoint, but rather seemed to be some nebulous factor that combined many facets of the very special man she felt she knew, but yet didn't know.

Restlessness kept her from sleep even though she could feel the need for it. Her thoughts were filled with the man who was occupying the couch in the living room just a few steps away. A soft thud distracted her for a second. Nastar had jumped up on the foot of the bed. But the distraction was immediately replaced by the memory of Egan's kiss. Joda felt her body flush with perilous warmth. She turned on her side, pulled her knees up together, rearranged the pillow under her head, then straightened out on her back again. Nastar reminded her, with a soft cry, that he was trying to sleep, and would rather do it undisturbed.

Joda stared into the darkness. The house was quiet, but there was an almost palpable tension in the air, and she could find no refuge from it. She looked at the bedside clock; an hour had passed since she had gotten into bed. Her throat felt dry. She was tired of staring at the ceiling; she eased out of bed without disturbing Nastar and headed for the kitchen and a glass of water.

The only sound in the living-dining area, which included the kitchen, was the soft crackling of the fire that still flickered as the last of the split log was consumed by hungry tongues of yellow-orange. Joda was careful not to add any other sound of her own as she filled a tilted glass from a barely running tap. She started back toward the bedroom, then stopped. Egan was asleep on the couch, still wearing the tan corduroy slacks and the tan-and-gray sweater he'd come in; he hadn't even bothered to pull the blanket over himself. It looked as if he'd taken a moment to relax before getting ready for bed, then fallen asleep unexpectedly.

Joda wondered if she should cover him; the room was still very warm from the fire, so she decided not to take a chance on disturbing his peaceful sleep. But she couldn't turn away from him. He looked so beautiful to her, the dim light from the fire illuminating the angular planes of his masculine features, the firm lines of his athletic body. One hand rested lightly just below his ribs, moving almost imperceptibly with each shallow breath. Such beautiful hands, the long fingers so artistically formed. Joda wanted to reach out and touch them. She moved closer to the couch; just standing close beside his sleeping figure delighted her. He stirred. Joda felt a prickle of alarm, though she was sure she hadn't disturbed him.

What would he say if he were to awaken and find her looking down at him? Would he be angry? Would he think her silly? Suddenly she felt as if she were standing there completely nude; she could feel her bare skin against the satin and lace of the brief teddy. Even in sleep, he could disturb her senses. She must leave his side before doing something foolish became imperative. Her legs felt weak as she backed away.

"Don't go, Joda."

His voice startled her. "Oh! I didn't mean to wake you."

"You didn't. Come here." He patted the cushion beneath him, pulled himself up and turned on his side to make room. "What's wrong, can't you sleep?"

She couldn't tell him what was really wrong. "I must have rested too much during the day," she said as she sat down beside him. "And I was thirsty." She held up the glass in her hand, feeling as if she needed to offer an excuse for being out of bed.

"The kitchen's over there," he said, a half-smile on his face as he pointed over his head.

"Well . . . I saw that you were uncovered. I thought I might . . ."

"Why didn't you? Cover me, that is."

"I didn't want to . . . disturb you. Egan, I'm . . ."

"You're disturbing me right now." He slid one hand up her back beneath her hair, sending shivers of delight up her spine. "Are you cold?" he asked with concern.

"No . . . not at all." He had felt her trembling.

His hand continued over her shoulder, lifting the thin strap with his finger. "This can't be keeping you very warm." His other hand came to rest on her thigh.

On the contrary! She was beginning to feel very

warm! "I should have put on my robe," she said shakily.

"Not on my account." His hand moved over the length of silken skin to her knee, then back up again, his fingers sliding to the inside of her leg. "I prefer the outfit you have on." In one deft stroke he moved her leg to one side as his fingers crept beneath the lacy high-cut leg.

"Oh!" The water glass slipped from her hand as his touch evoked a wave of fiery weakness. "Egan . . ."

"Let's not worry about that right now." His warm mouth was following the same path his hand had just taken.

The water she had just spilled left her thoughts completely as his teeth gently nipped at the sensitive skin of her inner thigh. She clutched at his back, convulsively grasping the soft wool of his sweater, feeling as if her desire for him was threatening her sanity. If only his fingers would stop their incredible assault. She wanted him to feel the same inescapable desire, but she could do nothing but hold on to him until the raging storm inside her burst free.

Joda leaned back against him as his hand retraced a path back along the inside of her thigh. Then she could feel him sit up beside her. She seemed to move in slow motion, her hands slipping under his sweater, then lifting it, with his help, up over his head. He got up, and as she watched, he finished undressing himself until he stood before her, gloriously unadorned except by extravagant desire.

"Come here, Egan," she breathed softly, reaching for him, arms outstretched to beckon him. Was it so selfish wanting so desperately to touch him? To feel the thrill of sinew and strength beneath her fingers, beneath her lips? Her hands slipped around his waist, her fingers finding the hollow curve at the base of his spine.

"Why do you have to be so beautiful, Egan?" she asked, her cheek snuggling his perfectly muscled frame. "I can't keep my hands away from you." Her fingertips began describing the taut roundness of his hips, pressing him closer to her.

"Joda . . ." he gasped as he felt himself straining against the voluptuous prison of her breasts.

"I'm so glad I got thirsty," she said with a smiling double-entendre. The vital masculine fragrance of him rose to her sensitive nostrils and made her quiver with excitement. She let her mouth trail a feathery line across his waist. Every muscle trembled as she nipped his tender skin with a gentle bite. "You feel so good," she whispered, letting her tongue flick out to taste him. She felt his hands tighten on her shoulders, then push away from her.

He knelt down on one knee before her, his eyes dark with hunger, and gently pulled the straps off her shoulders. The satiny top followed their downward course. The pressure of his hands on her breasts pushed her back until she was lying down full length on the couch. Then his hands slid down to help her out of the lacy bit of material.

Joda longed to taste him again, feeling deprived when he had pushed away from her, but then his lips were on hers satisfying her longing for him.

"I can't get enough of you, Joda," he groaned. "I can't . . ."

In the next instant Joda was filled with luxurious satisfaction and felt herself on the stormy edge of delicious release. The flames in the fireplace paled beside the pulsing fire-storm on the couch. Her knees came up on either side of him to hold him in the hungry bondage of her glistening silken thighs until, at last, they clung to one another, their passion spent in final glory.

They lay together in silence, their breathing beginning to calm, their heartbeats slowing. Egan eased his weight off her and adjusted his position so that he was sitting at her side, one hand on her breast. He leaned forward and kissed her tenderly. "I'm so glad you couldn't sleep," he said softly against her cheek, then lifted his eyes to hers.

"But you said I needed rest, Doctor," she said innocently.

"Malpractice, pure and simple. Will you sue, Miss Kerris?" Both hands were on her breasts now, teasing, dissipating what little strength she had left.

She grasped his wrists and stopped the movement. "I'll call my lawyer in the morning," she said, smiling. "Then we'll see what happens next."

He leaned forward and kissed the deep cleft between the rounded softness in his hands. "And the jury will believe anything you have to say, my beautiful Joda," he murmured against her sensitive skin. "I won't have a chance. I'm glad I have until morning to try to change your mind."

"About suing the doctor?"

He gathered her into his arms then, avoiding her question, pulling her first to a sitting position, then to her feet, ushering her ahead of him into the bedroom. "Let's get some sleep now, Joda. I want you ready for anything tomorrow."

"What do you mean, Egan?"

He didn't answer her until they had gotten into the

bedroom. "I heard the weather on the radio while driving up here this evening. Snowstorm. Sounds like it might be a big one."

"Oh? Well, we're used to that up here. We'll handle it."

Egan was right about the storm. In peaceful sleep, he and Joda were not even aware of its beginnings, but after breakfast Joda opened the curtains that hung at the sliding glass door and found the snow drifted almost halfway up the panes. With snow scrapers and gloved hands they unburdened Egan's white roadster, and Joda offered to help him put chains on for the trip down the mountain into Dillon, but Egan assured her it wasn't necessary. He had not only four-wheel drive but also all-weather tires.

Joda was right, too, about handling the storm—at least for a time. But even with a restful night's sleep spent snuggled warmly in Egan's arms, she was feeling a bit tired by midmorning. Once again she was teaching the beginning skiers, and the blowing snow and minus-twenty-degree wind-chill factor made the teaching difficult. Half of the students in the class of ten were children, and the youngsters always amazed her. They found the weather conditions no problem at all. But the five adults in the class were suffering from the cold and from being slightly out of shape. They were finding even the gradual slope of Checkerboard Flats an almost overwhelming challenge. Joda had stopped counting the number of times the operator had to stop the lift to accommodate their ineptness.

"Rough day," the lift operator said while they waited.

"Looks like Packsaddle lift is having one, too."

"It's the *lift* over there, not the skiers."

Joda took another look to her left. "That's the third time I've seen it stop. This is a bad day to be stranded in a chair."

The young man nodded. "Sitting can get mighty cold. I'll bet the complaints have already started."

He was correct in his assumption. Before going in to lunch, Joda spoke briefly to Rachel, who had been helping skiers get on the Packsaddle lift all morning, and she confirmed it. The complaints were pouring in.

Rachel pointed to a young boy, about fourteen, entering Mountain House. "And there goes another problem. He's about to lose his lift ticket, if I have anything to say about it."

"How's that?" Joda asked.

"Loves to swing the chairs. He gave the boys at the top quite a scare this morning. Had the chair swinging, and the lift stopped kind of abruptly just as he was getting off. I guess he took quite a fall, and the chair swung forward and hit him in the head to boot!"

All Joda could think about was another lawsuit. "Is he okay?"

"Oh, sure. The ski patrol was right on the spot. He's fine. It's everybody else that's shook-up. You know how Keystone is—anything and everything for the customer. Well, I'm glad to get a break. Have lunch with me?"

"Sure, I'd like that."

Mr. Birmingham had different ideas about her lunchtime activities, however. As soon as she entered Mountain House, he called her into his office. The tension of the morning did not ease as Joda sat down across from him. His expression was grave.

"Shelly Sloan's law firm has been in contact with Frank Seagle this morning. It seems she has a new proposal for us to consider."

Joda sat up a little straighter. The unrelieved tension of the morning continued to build.

"Ms. Sloan will drop the suit against the ski area if Keystone releases you as head ski instructor. With the amount of money involved, you can see how attractive an offer this is."

Good Lord! Hadn't Egan said the same thing just last night? Not quite the same words, but he had outlined exactly the same "proposal." Egan had called it an "exchange." The only outstanding difference between what Mr. Birmingham had just told her and what Egan had said the night before was that Egan had prefaced the idea with the words "what if."

"This is for real, right, Mr. Birmingham? This is not a 'we're-thinking-about-it' situation?"

"That's right, Joda," he said, and shifted his tall frame in the chair.

Joda could feel her anger trying to take control, and she suppressed it. This was not the time to waste the energy of her fury on her kindly boss. He had not been obligated to warn her about the possible course of events and he had no power to change them. But Joda suspected that Egan O'Neill did have that power. She suddenly felt chilled. She had been innocently playing right into their hands. Now those hands were about to crush her.

"What is there for me to do, Mr. Birmingham?"

"Right now, nothing." He shrugged. "Wait until

Keystone makes its decision. Then . . . I don't know." He was shaking his head forlornly.

"Thank you for confiding in me," Joda said as she stood to go. "I'm not going to lose hope. Maybe I'll get lucky somehow."

"I wouldn't bet on it, Joda," Mr. Birmingham replied gravely.

7

〜∾∾∾∾∾∾∾∾∿〜

Joda fought to stay in the present, to keep her mind focused on the task at hand. Her students seemed rested and refreshed after having their lunch, but her own thoughts were distracted. Even the weather seemed to be conspiring against her efforts to concentrate; by midafternoon the temperature had dropped another fifteen degrees and the snowfall had doubled, making her work twice as difficult.

She was also aware of continued problems with Packsaddle lift and wondered why no one had decided simply to close it down. Complimentary passes for another day could be given out and the loss might be less than losing the complaining skiers to another resort area.

The last run of the day brought Joda to the base of the mountain, and she bid good-bye and good luck to her exhausted charges. She had no idea how her evening would go, but she had the uneasy feeling that she would not be able to contain her anger at Egan O'Neill and might end up doing something very foolish, something probably—*very probably*—detrimental to her own situation. She shivered from the cold that usually didn't affect her at all. If only there were some distraction to claim her attention until she could calm down and begin to think rationally about the situation.

As if she had offered an answerable prayer, Packsaddle lift ground to another unplanned stop. She saw the lift operator pick up the phone as she hurried to Rachel to see if she could be of any help.

"This is it," Rachel said disgustedly. "I'm quitting. I can't listen to another complaint today."

"It'll be going again in just a minute, Rachel," Joda assured her. "Johnny's on the spot."

"Humph," was Rachel's disgruntled reply.

Her pessimism was well-founded. It took Johnny only a couple of minutes to discover that the lift had run for the last time today; the brake had frozen solid.

A rude wind played havoc with the chill factor, and Joda could hear the voices of skiers who were stranded on the lift chairs. Many were uncomplimentary.

"Let's go! I'm freezing!"

"Get this heap moving!"

"Just let me off this contraption. I'll teach you how to run it right!"

She knew from long experience that very soon, when it became apparent that the lift was stopped for good, people would begin to consider the possibility of jumping or climbing off. She knew the ski patrol had already been alerted to the situation, but the minutes it would take them to get the evacuation procedures under way would give the stranded skiers time to think about trying to rescue themselves. The combination of fear and freezing temperatures could addle the brain.

"I'm going to take Checkerboard lift up and see if I can help from there," she told Rachel as she started back toward the wide easy beginner slope of Checkerboard Flats. Just a few minutes ago she thought she'd taken that lift for the last time today; this time her destination would be different. She would leave the chair and turn left onto the expert slope, Go Devil, and from there she could cross to the treacherous terrain beneath Packsaddle lift.

As she rode the chair lift that would take her only a short distance up the mountain, she remembered her first experience with a real emergency evacuation. It had happened on the first day of her testing to become a ski instructor. During her training they had practiced rescue procedures, but the real thing had turned out to be a horrifying experience.

Joda had not been a rescuer; she'd been a victim. Suspended high above the almost unnegotiable chute of deep and undulating powder under the lift, and whipped by bone-chilling wind currents, she had experienced strange tricks of the mind. Intellectually, she knew the distance to the ground was much too great for a safe jump down, but as she and her chair partner waited, the distance seemed to shrink, and after a quarter of an hour the jump looked as if it would be as easy as taking the last step off a staircase.

Joda remembered thinking that her rationalizations were probably exclusive to her own mind, until, to her horror, a man in the chair ahead of hers took the plunge to the ground. She could still hear his shriek of pain as he landed; both his legs were broken. It happened more often than she liked to think about.

"Hurry up, darn it," she said aloud to Checkerboard lift, and the girl sitting next to her gave her a surprised look. "Pardon me?" she asked.

Joda had forgotten she wasn't alone. "Oh. Excuse

me. Nothing." Thankfully, the ride was over and she wouldn't have to explain.

With great respect for its difficulty and the speeding skiers using it, Joda crossed Go Devil, then threaded her way among the tall pines that lined the slope and Packsaddle. The mountain soared above her almost a thousand feet to the top of the lift.

Just as she arrived, Mike, one of the ski partrol, appeared at the top of a small rise farther up the steep slope carrying a coil of heavy rope attached to a metal seat, the evacuation platform. He called out to the stranded skiers, "We'll be rescuing you shortly. Please stay where you are. Stay calm." He moved to the support pole nearest to where Joda was standing and dropped his burden.

"It's gonna take more than *him* to get us out of here!" Joda heard a fear-tinged voice say above her.

"Where's the fire department?"

"Yeah! We need a hook and ladder up here."

"Shut up, Hector!" a woman's voice commanded.

"Just a few more minutes, folks," Mike called out. "Stay where you are," he reminded them again as he moved on down the line of chairs and tried to reassure the anxious people.

Joda knew each minute that passed by would seem like an hour to those above her. With the wind-chill factor hovering around thirty degrees below zero, fingers and toes would begin to stiffen, then ache painfully, and faces would redden and start to feel as if they would crack with any change of expression. The people had already been sitting still for about ten minutes; it would be another ten minutes or so before Mike returned with his three helpers. Her main concern would be trying to keep the skiers calm during their wait.

137

"Hey, lady! Come on up here. It's time we got acquainted." The young man who had shouted was leaning precariously forward in his seat.

"Please sit back, sir," Joda told him in a loud but pleasant voice. She could see that the woman who sat beside him was fearfully gripping the armrests with mittened hands, and she didn't want anyone getting panicky.

The man apparently could see the advantage of taking her advice and straightened himself in the chair. Joda slipped her skis off, planted them tail-down in the snow, then started walking slowly up the hill. Most of the people were talking quietly among themselves, and with the wind, it was almost impossible to hear what they were saying to one another. No problems yet, she thought. Most of the skiers on Packsaddle were, no doubt, experts headed for the top of Go Devil. They would probably remain coolheaded through the rescue procedures. It was the beginners, on their way to Last Chance and Schoolmarm, that worried her. They were looking down at some of the most perilous snow-covered earth on the mountain, and the idea of trying to negotiate it after they had been retrieved from the lift was even more frightening to them than the rescue itself.

Joda heard a shout. "Hey! Anyone have a deck of cards?" It was the young man who had yelled at her before, dressed in Levi's, ski jacket, and a cowboy hat that gave his ears no protection at all. His disruptive remarks were probably influenced by the arctic cold and nervousness. Joda couldn't blame him for trying to distract his own attention from his painful plight.

Before she could turn and address him, another voice was heard. "Why don't you shut up, kid?" a deep male voice snarled.

Joda tensed; the nervousness seemed to be catching. She started back toward the trouble.

The young man twisted around, looking back over his shoulder at the man in the chair behind him. "What's the matter with you, mister? Can't you see the humor in this?" He laughed loudly for all to hear.

"Listen, kid—"

"Or are you scared?"

"Calm down, folks," Joda said in her most authoritative voice, projecting the order easily over the moaning wind. "Let's not get upset."

"That's easy for *you* to say," the man returned rudely. "I'm paying a fortune—and for what?"

He had every right to be frustrated, especially if he'd been on the lift any of the other times it had stopped today, but his surly manner was introducing an unnecessary extra tension into an already uneasy situation.

"I'm getting out of here," Joda heard him say to his chair companion, a woman.

"No! Don't do that!" the woman yelled.

Joda looked up just in time to see the man reach down and release one ski.

"Look out below," the woman screamed.

"Runaway ski," Joda shouted at the top of her voice.

Another two steps and Joda would have been directly under the falling missile. She watched as it caromed down the steep incline and prayed no one was standing below her, out of sight. Luckily, the thin strip of fiberglass slammed into one tree and then stopped against another.

"Sir. *Sir!*" Joda yelled. "Don't drop your other ski, sir." She was trying to sound respectful and assertive at the same time. Somehow, she had to stay in control

of the situation until the ski patrol arrived. She moved
directly under the man's chair. Hopefully, her position
would deter the release of his other ski.

"Move out of the way, girl. I'm getting off this thing
one way or another. Now, stand back!"

"Just a few more minutes, sir."

"I'm not waiting," he growled, and leaned forward
to release his other ski.

"No!" Joda took three quick steps down the hill
before the ski began its descent. When it hit the
ground it landed on its side, then flattened and shot
toward her. All she could do was fall forward and hope
to land on it to stop it. She hit the ground. A cheer rose
above her. The deadly weapon was pinned beneath
her and everyone who had seen what had happened
was loudly applauding her efforts. Even the man who
had dropped the ski was looking back at her, an
expression of disbelief on his face. She could have
gladly wrung his neck.

She could feel relieved for only a second. The very
fact that the man had dropped his other ski clearly
meant that he planned to take the next logical step and
jump from the lift. She couldn't take the time to
wonder about what was motivating him to do such a
dangerous thing. She had to act, and quickly.

Joda grasped the ski beneath her, stood, and
planted it in the ground. When she looked up, she saw
that the woman next to him was holding his ski poles
as well as her own and was talking animatedly to him
as he slid forward on the seat. There was only one
course of action to take; she had to make him think
that his rescue was imminent and immediate.

"Wait!" she shouted at him. "Let me help you."

He paused in his forward motion and looked down
to see Joda rushing toward the base of the tower

directly in front of his chair. Hopefully he wouldn't realize that she couldn't do the job alone, at least not until help actually arrived.

Joda slung the heavy coil of thick rope over one shoulder, adjusted the weight of the rescue seat behind her, and started up the tall black tower. Her progress was deliberately slow; she wanted to give the ski patrol as much time as she could. As she approached the midway point on the tower, she could see the man's expression. It did not reflect fear. He was angry!

Joda stopped for a moment in her upward climb, pretended to adjust the equipment she carried. Out of the corner of her eye she could see that he was not dressed properly—woolen gloves, probably soaked through and freezing, a cross-country ski jacket too lightweight for alpine skiing. His cheeks and nose were bright red. He was a tall man, and heavy; his rescue would not be easy.

"Quit stalling, lady! Can't you see we're in trouble up here?"

Joda's tension increased. A fearful person was much easier to deal with than an angry one. Fear could be reasoned with most times, but anger was a different story altogether, many times unreasonable and illogical. *Hurry, Mike!* She continued her intentionally slow climb to the top of the cable tower.

The equipment she carried and her hastily decided course of action were doing the job. From the moment she had picked up the rope from the ground where Mike had left it and started her climb, the man had not threatened to do anything foolish. *Just a few more minutes!* She reached the top. Normally the rope would have been allowed to play out into the hands of someone on the ground. In this situation, however, she had the entire coil to deal with and could make a great show of the unwieldy nature of the equipment. It took her several minutes to separate the proper strand from the rest and lift the rescue seat over the cable.

As the chair swung over the cable, Joda momentarily lost her grip on the attached rope and the chair dropped toward the ground. Even though there was no one in the chair, she heard a gasp of fear, probably from the woman. Joda stopped the falling seat easily and began to haul it back up, but the incident had tipped her hand.

"I don't think you can handle this, lady!" the man shouted angrily. "If you think I'm getting on that contraption and get dropped on my can, you've got another thing coming!" He started to edge forward in the chair again.

"No! Wait!"

Mike and three others with the ski patrol appeared at the top of the knoll upslope. Joda had never been happier to see anyone.

Mike sized up the situation quickly. "Stay calm, folks," his rich baritone voice commanded with confidence. "We'll have you out of here in just a few minutes." He motioned for Joda to toss the rope to one of the men beside him, then stopped under the man's chair.

"Out of the way, son. I'm coming down."

Joda thought she could feel a wave of panic flow through the stranded skiers. If the man jumped and were badly injured, it could delay the rescue procedures. These people were freezing.

"Hey, mister! You'd better stay put!" It was the young man in the chair ahead of the tower.

"Yeah! You're wastin' time, mister. Let 'em do their

job." The people were beginning to realize their jeopardy.

Joda checked beneath her. The rope, angling up-slope a few feet from the side of the tower, was now firmly wrapped around the waist of the man on the ground. He nodded to her.

"Sir, the chair's going to slide toward you. Then I'll lower it," Joda said in a loud voice. He looked toward her as she gave the rope several practice flicks. When it was directly in front of the chair, she lowered it slowly to him, wondering as she did so if he would allow the woman to go down first. He didn't, but the woman didn't seem to mind. The expression on her face clearly showed that she would be happy to be rid of him even if it meant delaying her own rescue.

Joda instructed the man in soothing tones, and as soon as she was sure that he had the seat firmly under his buttocks, she began to briefly explain what was going to take place. Without waiting for her to finish, and without any warning, he abruptly launched himself off the chair lift.

The patrol man below was exceptionally strong and well-braced, but the speed with which the man left the chair put an extraordinary burden on his stability. He slid forward and the rope began to slip through his hands. With superhuman effort he was able to stop the fall, but the now swinging burden was a tremendous drain on his strength. Joda was moving down the tower, her presence no longer needed at the top. She watched warily as the man began to move toward the ground once more. Then he was falling again!

Joda knew that with a strong leap she could reach the rope—if she didn't miss it and if she could hold on, her extra weight would stop the man's fall. Her reactions took over; without a second thought for her own safety, she reflexively pushed off the iron step.

The rope was burning in her hands as she tried to grip it tightly enough to stop her own sliding descent. Another cheer rose above her. There were three people on the controlling line now, her hands were holding her, and the danger was past. The next few seconds passed in a blur for her as she slid down inch by inch, then dropped to the ground. The man was safely down, and so was she.

Without a thank-you and without bothering to retrieve his skis, the angry man stomped away toward Go Devil, cursing loudly. The ski patrol was in control now. Thankfully, she could leave the area too, unless for some reason they needed her further. Mike assured her that they did not. Amid profuse thanks and cheerful applause, Joda donned her skis and disappeared into the trees.

Now that the crisis was past, she tried to relax. Her instantaneous reaction to the impending disaster had left no time for reflection, but now, as she skied toward Mountain House, the full weight of what she had done flooded her senses and she began to wonder at the risk she'd taken. Her superb physical condition and training had helped her avoid certain calamity, but she realized that luck had played an important part in her success, too, and she knew she never wanted to be in the same situation.

A broad smile crossed her face as she remembered wishing for a distraction from her worries. With this kind of distraction, who *needed* other troubles? But her smile lasted only seconds. She did, indeed, have other troubles. The incident had pointedly directed her attention to the fact that she was exceptionally good at her job and *should* be considered an indispensable part of Keystone's staff. The evaluation was her own, of course, but by the time she reached the bottom of the ski slope, she was angrier than the man she had just rescued, angrier than she had ever been in her life. *How dare they even consider firing me!*

She left the ski area hurriedly, her progress toward home hampered by the heavy snow; but the rented compact behaved well on the slippery roads and got her to Aspenwalk safely. In a state of agitation she started a fire and put the teakettle on to boil. She thought her trials had started on the first day she had met Egan O'Neill, but she realized on her way home that they were actually just now beginning. Uncharacteristically, Joda had allowed others to manipulate her life—first Shelly Sloan, then Egan O'Neill, even Frank Seagle through her trust in him. She had unconsciously delegated control to these people because of the anomalous nature of the situation. But that was all over now. Tonight she would take back the reins of her life.

As soon as Nastar was fed, Joda fixed herself a light meal and began to plan as she ate it. Her life had to go on in its usual fashion, and her work, if she still had a job, would necessarily take up most of her time. But in the hours she had left, she was going to do her very best to find a solution to her enthrallment.

Egan had said this morning that he would get her car back to her, but she would take care of that herself, tonight. She had lived without him for almost twenty-seven years; sadly, she would now resume that exclusivity. As for Mr. Birmingham, another thank-you was in order for his warning, but she would also try to solicit his help in taking her side opposing whatever forces might appear against her. Surely her loyalty and good record were worth that much.

Next she would inform Frank Seagle that her energies were at his service in his investigation of Shelly Sloan. If he refused her help, she would feel free to do some investigating on her own. She had no idea where to start, but she was determined to find out the reason for Shelly's uncommon antagonism toward her.

Joda finished her meal, changed clothes, then called Jack to make sure he would be at the garage until she got there. The drive was slow and tense because of the continuing storm, but the highway was well-traveled and fairly clear. In Golden there was no storm at all.

"Young fella called today . . . said he'd pick your car up *tomorrow*. Change of plans, Joda?"

She nodded.

"You can use my phone if you want," he said.

"No, thanks, Jack. I'll let him know later." But her deceit was inconsistent with her usual behavior and extremely uncomfortable. Earlier she'd had no intention of informing him at all, but she would have to confront him eventually. She was feeling good about her decisions up to this point. Why not get it over with tonight?

"I've changed my mind, Jack. Thanks. I *will* use your phone."

Egan was surprised to hear from her, but delighted to meet her at Simm's Landing in Golden for a glass of wine. By the time she arrived at the hillside restaurant, she was trembling with anxiety. She had never been the victim of such beguiling delusion before, had no idea how she would handle the confrontation, but knew that she must. Egan arrived about ten minutes after she did and found her at a secluded table for two. She had already ordered and paid for two glasses of white wine.

He sat down and immediately took both her hands in his. "This is such a pleasant surprise, Joda. Did you know that this is the first time you've ever called me?"

Joda stiffened in her chair and withdrew her hands. "I'm afraid it will be the last time, too, Mr. O'Neill."

His frown was instant. "Why? I don't understand."

"You will, I'm sure, as soon as I explain it." She paused for a second to gather her courage. "I don't like being lied to, Egan. Last night you pretended not to know what Shelly Sloan might do next, but as it turns out, you had some pretty accurate guesses. A little *too* accurate as far as I'm concerned." Now that the confrontation had begun, she was feeling calmer.

"What has she done?" he asked quietly.

Joda could almost believe he didn't know. Almost. "Please don't pretend ignorance anymore. I've had it with your innocent act and I don't believe you're off the case, either." Her words sounded cruel to her ear, but she felt more in control.

"What makes you think I lied to you about that?" he asked.

"Because today Shelly Sloan proposed the exact 'exchange' you outlined last night: she'll back off if she gets my head on a platter."

"I really *was* guessing, Joda. Think about it for a minute. Why would I deliberately give away a client's game plan? I could be disbarred for divulging privileged information."

What he was saying was entirely possible, but on the other hand . . . "Maybe your strategy wasn't discussed until this morning. In which case the decision couldn't be considered privileged information at the time you mentioned it to me."

Egan seemed to be impressed with her line of thinking, looking at her with new respect, but he persisted in proclaiming his innocence. "Joda, why would I suggest quitting your job except to protect you?"

"That's simple," she said suspiciously. "If I quit my job without a hassle, not only would Shelly's bizarre wish for my destruction be fulfilled but also she could proceed with her lawsuit. Think about *that*, Mr. O'Neill."

"You're right," he said quietly.

"You bet I'm right, but it's no consolation, believe me."

"And all I can do is deny any knowledge of what Shelly has done." There was disappointment in his deep voice. "How can I make you believe me, Joda?"

"I don't think you can," she said softly and with a tone of finality. "And you won't be getting another chance. You said I'd become a pawn. Well, I'm not yours anymore, and no one else is going to use me again. I know I can't order you out of my life because this lawsuit is probably going to keep throwing us together, but I'm not going to let you and Shelly Sloan destroy my life. I'm going to fight this. I'm sure there must be some legal recourse for me if I'm fired without just cause."

"Joda, I don't want to see you hurt."

Joda steeled herself against his specious sincerity. "I've already been hurt as deeply as you could possibly imagine, Egan. At least Shelly's intentions are perfectly clear and exposed, even if her motivations are not. I can deal with that better than I can deal with your deceit.''

She had come down really hard on him and couldn't imagine what his reaction might be. Anger, very likely. An explanation, hopefully.

Egan's hands slid off the table and into his lap as he leaned against the back of his chair.

The silence was dreadful. Joda had expected him to at least be angry. Fear crept into a corner of her mind.

Finally he looked down at his hands for a moment, then brought them back up on the table, placing his fingers on the stem of the wineglass before him. He began slowly to turn the goblet around and around on its central axis.

Have I made a mistake? she wondered frantically. Has he been telling the truth all along? Had she acted too hastily and judged him wrongly again? Last night her heart had told her she was falling in love with him, and yet now she was treating him like he was her most fearsome enemy. A war between conflicting ideas raged inside her. What choices did she have?

If she succumbed to his apparent concern and sensitivity and then was *wrong* about how much he cared, her heart could be incontrovertibly broken beyond repair. And if he had been and still *was* playacting to obtain her trust, she could jeopardize whatever kind of successful future she might ever have dreamed of.

On the other hand, if he had been telling the truth all along, and she refused to believe him, she could lose the friendship of the most precious man she had ever met. If she really did mean something to him and she rejected him, who would care for *his* "tender heart" as he had said he cared for hers?

It was imperative that she make up her mind. Both her heart and her future were at stake. A moment ago she had accused him of deceit, and he had not denied it; no explanations had been offered. Sad . . . but her life was better off in her own hands.

"I have to go now, Egan." Joda stood up, leaving her wine untouched. She turned, retrieved her down jacket from the back of the chair and put it on. He was looking at her now as she picked up her purse. "I'm leaving now," she said again. "Good-bye."

He stood, his abrupt movement startling her. "This is *not* good-bye." Strong fingers grasped her upper arm, and he propelled her quickly and forcefully out of the restaurant and to her car. With a hand on each arm, he held her in place against the side of the car. "I have a lot of things to do before I can see you again." He spoke forcefully.

Hasn't he heard anything I've said? "Egan, don't you understand? It's over."

He gave her a shake. "No," he said sharply. "It *isn't* over. It's *you* who don't understand any of this. Now, go home!" He released her and abruptly left her standing there.

She couldn't believe what had just happened. He had dismissed her as he might dismiss a hostile witness.

"Good-bye!" she spat into the silent night around her, then softly, her eyes filling with tears, "Good-bye, my love."

8

Highway Seventy west was rapidly glazing and the little coupe's headlights illuminated hypnotic swirls of crystal brightness. Joda was having trouble concentrating; the image of Egan's face stared at her through the foggy windshield. Before she realized it, the car's back wheels started to oscillate in an ever-widening arc. Her mind leaped back into the present time, and she began trying to steer in the direction she wanted to go. In what seemed like slow motion, the car spun around in a full circle. Joda tapped on the accelerator pedal. In an eternity of seconds the front-wheel drive finally responded to her expert manipulations, but Joda was trembling uncontrollably; her whole life, not just her car, seemed out of control. She pulled to the side of the highway, set the emergency brake, then slumped forward over the steering wheel.

She doubled her fist and slammed it against the dashboard. It was *so* important to be happy with one's life. She *had* to get on with her plans, and this frightening episode made life seem all the more precious, her plans all the more urgent.

* * *

A few embers remained in the fireplace, and with a little attention she had a fire going again. It was so good to be home. Nastar followed her to the phone and sat on her lap as she dialed Mr. Birmingham's number.

"Congratulations on your rescue today," he said right away. "Mr. Harris Forrester is a lucky man."

"Yes, isn't he?" She paused; then: "Mr. Birmingham, I wanted to thank you again for confiding in me today."

"It was the least I could do, Joda."

"Just sparing me that sort of surprise was a blessing, believe me."

"Sounds like you're taking it well."

"I haven't resigned myself to losing my job, if that's what you mean. In fact, that's the other reason I called. I've been invaluable to the ski area in many ways, not only in my teaching but also in public relations and goodwill, and I'm asking for your help. In case it's necessary, I want you to speak up for me."

There was no sound from his end of the phone for several seconds. Then: "I'm not sure I'd be of any help, Joda."

"Mr. Birmingham—"

"But I *am* on your side in this," he added quickly. "For what it's worth."

"That's all I can ask, Mr. Birmingham," she said. "I'll let you know if there's anything specific you can do. I'll see you tomorrow. Good-bye."

She fixed herself a cup of tea before making the next call.

"Frank Seagle's residence," an elderly man said, then assured Joda that Mr. Seagle would be right along.

"I heard about your heroics today," Frank began without saying hello. "Mr. B. told me. Congrats. Great job."

"Thank you," she said lightly; then: "I want to ask you a question, Frank."

"Shoot."

"If I'm fired, would I have any legal recourse?" Again she had a silent partner on the other end of the phone for several seconds. Instantly Joda realized what a mistake she had made in calling him. Frank was a corporate lawyer; if she were to be fired, she would be on the opposite side of the fence. Frank would be her adversary, not her advocate.

He confirmed: "I'm not in a position to advise you, Joda." But he hurried to add, "But it has nothing to do with my opinion of you. Don't ever think that."

"I shouldn't have asked," she said bluntly. "But I want to offer my time. I know you're trying to find out what's motivating Shelly Sloan, and I want you to call me if I can help in any way. I have a personal interest, you know."

There was another pause. "I understand. Thank you for offering. Perhaps I will."

"Thank you, Frank. 'Bye for now."

Intuitively she knew he would not call her for help. The decision to release her might already have been made, but regardless, her own investigation of Shelly Sloan would proceed on Monday. She *had* to help herself if she could.

Next morning she had no sooner stepped into Mountain House than she was surrounded by several of the employees, all with their own copy of the Dillon *Daily,* all talking at once, congratulating her on her heroics of the afternoon before. Joda was confused until Betty handed her a paper.

There had been a photographer on the ski lift two chairs back from Harris Forrester and he had recorded the rescue on film, then given the story to the *Daily*. The photo showed Joda a split second before her hands had grasped the rope after her jump from the tower, and the description of the rescue was accurate down to the last detail. The writer, without libeling himself, had skillfully described Mr. Forrester's crude and dangerous behavior while keeping others waiting, freezing in their lift chairs. Joda smiled to herself, imagining what the antagonistic Mr. Forrester would do when he read it. She had wanted to slap him in the face, herself.

It seemed that almost everyone was aware of what had happened yesterday afternoon. The piece had been in the Denver Post, as well, and one of her students brought her a copy of it after lunch. Joda hadn't felt this popular since the airing of her "Ski Tips" television series at the beginning of the season. The recognition felt good.

At the end of the day, Joda found a message to see Mr. Birmingham in his office before she left for home. She was ready for bad news, but was thoroughly surprised when he greeted her with a broad smile and a warm handshake of congratulation.

"Well, you've done it again, Joda," he began enthusiastically. "The name of Keystone is on everyone's lips because of you. Sit down, sit down." He pointed to the chair across from his as he sat down himself. "We couldn't have gotten any better publicity if we'd paid an expensive advertising firm to put us in the limelight." He leaned forward in his chair. "And listen to this. One of the television stations from Denver is coming up here tomorrow morning at nine to do an interview for tomorrow night's local news. What do you think of that?"

Her pride in a job well done notwithstanding, Joda wasn't sure how she felt about it. "That's very nice, Mr. Birmingham," she said with little enthusiasm. Her mind was busy racing ahead, trying to figure out how this exceptional good fortune could be used to her advantage.

"You don't sound too excited about it," he said curiously. "In this day and age, ski areas can use all the favorable press they can get. This is a gem of an opportunity for Keystone to shine." He paused. "And for you to look good, too," he added almost as an afterthought.

"Well, I don't know . . ."

"You're not going to say no, are you, Joda? You'll do it, won't you?"

Joda sat quietly for a moment. Whatever she was going to do had to be to her own best advantage. She had two choices: refuse or agree. Refusing was out of the question, and she nodded her assent. There would be many ways to handle such an interview. Before tomorrow she would have to give the various possibilities all her attention. "How long do you think it will take?"

"An hour ought to be plenty of time."

"I'll be here."

"Joda, we need this." He had a worried look on his face. "You don't have any qualms about doing it, do you?"

Was he beginning to realize, as she was, what a great amount of power was being delegated to her? Keystone would be at her mercy, and the media were not such that they would pass up a good story if she decided to tell them what was really happening to her. Would she? "I can't say exactly how I feel about it."

But later, she knew exactly how she felt and what she would do. The interviewer was an acquaintance of hers. Keystone would shine, all right, but so would Joda Kerris, and the *public* would see it firsthand.

The interview turned out to be a simple operation that took less than fifteen minutes. They stood at the base of the mountain near the machinery that ran the Packsaddle lift. The camera was angled up the mountain so that the moving lift chairs and the people riding them could be seen. Dennis had been briefed and had agreed enthusiastically to Joda's angle on the story. He was a friend. The taping went smoothly and just as Joda intended.

The description of the rescue went particularly well, with Mike, from the ski patrol, lending firsthand credibility to the fantastic story of Joda's leap for Mr. Forrester's safety, maybe for his life. The drama of the piece was greatly enhanced by Dennis' questions leading his viewers to the inevitable conclusion that Keystone was, in all ways, a wonderful place to be . . . and a safe one.

"I guess there's not a lot more anybody can say about the dedication and talents of this fine crew here at Keystone. Joda, we've known each other for about three years now. I can remember when you first became head instructor here. There were some skeptics, weren't there?"

"Yes, Dennis, there were."

"Is it tough getting to be a head ski instructor, Joda?"

"It's a lot of hard work and training . . . but if you

love the work, it's all worth it . . . even if you do have to go through some difficult times."

"What was the hardest thing you had to do?"

"I had to convince a lot of people that I could do the job."

"Well! I'll bet you're not worrying about *that* anymore!"

"Keystone took a chance on me, Dennis—"

"And you've never let them down! I'm proud to know you, Joda Kerris." His hand touched her shoulder. "Is there anything else exciting going on in your life that we should know about? We want to keep your fans happy, you know!"

"Not a thing, Dennis. Not a thing." She smiled sweetly. She had accomplished her mission and now she would wait and see what she had gained.

"Joda, Mike, thank you for letting us share this exciting story with you." The camera focused in on a one-shot of Dennis. "And now we're going to show you just a few of the exciting things that are happening here on Keystone Mountain." The camera shut off.

"Do you have all the shots you need, Tracy?" Dennis asked the woman behind the camera.

"Everything."

"That's a wrap, then. Mike, thanks again." He shook Mike's hand. "Joda, thank you, too. I guess I'll see you when you do your 'Ski Tips' again, if not before. I'm looking forward to it."

"So am I, Dennis. Thanks . . . for everything." She gave him a hug before he walked away.

Although Joda thought her popularity would fade as soon as yesterday's newspaper was thrown into the trash, it did not. People were asking to be in her classes—"insisting" would probably have been a better word—and they filled quickly to capacity. Her classes were seldom small, but she couldn't help but remember back to the day when she had had a class of one—Egan O'Neill. Even with all the attention she was getting, she found it impossible to get the man out of her mind, no matter how hard she tried. She supposed there was only one thing that would clear him out of her thoughts, and that was time. She couldn't help wishing that enough of it had already passed to ease the pain she was feeling.

9

~000000000~

Joda awoke to bright sunshine and a feeling that
everything was going to turn out all right. She hurried
through her exercises and other preparations for the
day, her mind on the task ahead of her. She would go
to the main library in Denver and search for clues in
their files of old newspapers. She had decided that if
Shelly's family were as wealthy and well known as
Frank had intimated, there would be something about
the accident that had taken their lives. Not that she
had any idea how their death might be affecting
Shelly's behavior; intuition was guiding her. All she
had to go on was the approximate date of their death,
and she was prepared to stay in the library for the
entire two days she had off if that were necessary. She
hoped it wouldn't be.

The newspapers of seven years ago were filled with
stories that might have kept Joda intrigued for hours,
but under the pressure of time, she hurried past them
to the obituaries. It wasn't until she had gone through
an entire year's worth of daily papers that she realized

she might be looking for the wrong name. It was just possible that Shelly had been married during that time or that her father had actually been her stepfather. A new idea had to be tried.

What had Frank told her about Shelly and her family? Her parents had died in some sort of accident seven years ago. Shelly had been twenty-four, rising within her field as a teacher of dance. Shelly had quit her job to care for her fifteen-year-old brother. Frank hadn't told her his name. Should she call him? Probably not.

Shelly's brother had been a rebellious teenager, difficult to handle, going out without permission and without informing anyone where he would be. A skiing accident had claimed his life. What had Frank said about that? "On the day it happened, Shelly didn't even know where he was. She found out from the newspaper the next day."

Joda decided to take a chance with the newspapers of that particular period of recent history. One obituary column after another passed before her eyes. She became obsessed with names that started with an S. The Smiths, the Smathers, the Singletons were all catching her eye and stealing her time. By noon she was tiring and frustrated. Perhaps she *should* call Frank Seagle.

She left the microfilm reader for a nearby phone, picked it up and dialed six of the seven digits of his number, then hung up. No, she thought, I'm not going to ask him another question. I don't need to hear his refusal to advise me again. Also, there was no way of knowing if Keystone had made the decision to fire her, and she certainly didn't want to hear such news over the phone. She called her Aunt Hally instead and invited herself to dinner and an overnight stay, then returned to her newspapers.

The next two hours passed more tediously than the first; Joda's mind began to wander a bit as a certain malaise descended about her. She began reading the sports page on the chance that it might have something and to give her reading variety. The diversion helped to freshen her for the next assault on the wearisome task.

There was an inside page of the sports section in front of her, an article on how some amateur skiers practiced for the Nastar races. The subject interested her for two reasons. One, Keystone held daily Nastar races, and two, Joda had given many racing clinics for amateurs. The writer described the videotape analysis of the races and a coin-operated racing system that allows a skier to try to beat his own time through practice runs.

Intrigued by the complimentary references to Keystone's contribution to amateur ski racing, Joda turned to the next page to read the rest of the article. Just to the right of the continued column a familiar face caught her eye. It was a picture of John Raynald, taken just about two weeks before his twenty-first birthday. The article was an account of his death.

Joda sat back in her chair, stunned, not believing that what she had just read could possibly be the truth. But why would they have printed it otherwise? She had met John Raynald on the day of his twentieth birthday, on a bright and sunny November morning that had brought him to Keystone for his first skiing lesson.

He had known the most basic rudiments, self-taught or encouraged by his friends. But his interest in skiing was growing and he wanted to polish his skills by taking lessons. All this he explained to her, and more. His family did not approve of his participation in the sport; he said they thought it too dangerous for a talented violinist. He was in college, still living at home, and he tried to keep peace as best he could. When skiing, those at home believed him to be somewhere else.

Joda remembered wondering at the time how on earth a twenty-year-old could live at home under such conditions. As she learned more about the young man, she realized that the members of his family, whoever they were, were apparently demanding and overprotective to an absurd degree, but they were paying the bills. He was keeping them happy the best way he knew how—by staying in school, by practicing and by lying.

John Raynald had been a handsome young man. Joda had liked him and had come to treat him like a younger brother. They had had fun together and shared their enjoyment of skiing whenever John could find the time for lessons. However, one aspect of their acquaintance had marred Joda's enjoyment of it, and finally destroyed it.

After about three months John Raynald had believed himself to be in love with Joda, and it was then that the relationship had begun to disintegrate. When John realized that Joda wasn't romantically interested, he began to do everything in his power to attract her attention. In February she had assured him that though she wanted to continue being his friend, she had nothing more in mind than that.

With all the fervor and determination of the young, John worked diligently to show his ultimate worth and prove that what he felt for her was not "puppy love."

He skipped days' worth of classes so that he could ski and enter the amateur Nastar competitions. He raced with anyone and everyone who would agree to give him a good run, and week after grueling week he was convinced, despite Joda's protestations, that he had gained another minim of her respect and interest.

It didn't take John long to get the reputation of the craziest downhill racer on the mountains of the Summit, Keystone and Arapahoe Basin, Breckenridge, and Copper Mountain. By mid-March the story was that he would take any chance, no matter how daring, to win any race. And he challenged everyone.

At first Joda thought his efforts laudable; he was her star pupil. But it became apparent that his purpose was to impress her. No matter what it took, he was going to shine in her eyes. As the weeks went by, she talked to him, raced with him and let him win, tried to reason with him, but to no avail. He was convinced that the better skier he was, the more certain Joda was to love him. Finally Joda had to tell him good-bye.

As far as she knew, he had never come back to Keystone Mountain again. For a time his reputation followed him from mountain to mountain around the Summit during the final days of the season, and then, just as spring skiing was coming to a close, she stopped hearing about him altogether.

She looked at the reader screen before her, at the handsome face peering from it, and read the article in its entirety. Joda had to imagine how the impromptu race must have begun—a challenge; an insult; a provoking, perhaps embarrassing comment. John had become an expert at goading people into a contest. His last one had taken place on the second day of skiing in November, on a particularly difficult slope at Copper Mountain.

At approximately sixty-five miles an hour, headed straight down the fall line, John had lost control, plummeting forward down the fearsome incline. His neck had been broken; he had died instantly.

As Joda read, her hand moved to the thin line of a scar along her jawline. Except for that one fleeting moment when she had been in the pool with Egan and he had asked her about the scar, it had been over a year since she had thought about John Raynald at all. Had Egan known? Impossible! How could he? And then she saw it. "Survived by a sister, Shelly Sloan."

Bits and pieces of her conversation with Frank Seagle began coming back to her. Of course! Why hadn't she been able to at least suspect some sort of a connection? The answer to that question was simple—Egan O'Neill. Since he had come into her life she had been able to think of little else. That, my dear, she said to herself, will never happen again!

Joda straightened; she was thinking clearly now. There were other past incidents that fit into the pattern of events influencing her life right now. John's secretiveness about his family, his reluctance to talk about them at all, except to say they were paying the bills to forge his obligation to them. His resentment had probably caused his silence . . . or could it have been his mourning and his sorrow? He had lost his parents; perhaps they'd been beloved. Had he thought that Shelly had loved him less? Perhaps Shelly had never let him forget what sacrifices she had made for him. Joda remembered now, too, that when Shelly had her accident, she had accused Joda of causing all her life problems. Joda had told Egan she had dismissed Shelly's words as the ravings of a person in great pain. Had Egan known, even then, the reasons behind

Shelly's plan? Joda felt a stab of pain in her chest. *Don't let that be true!*

It took her another hour to find the Raynald name again in another obituary column. Mr. and Mrs. Daniel Randolf Raynald had died in November, seven years and four months ago . . . on the day of their son's fifteenth birthday. In the same paper she found an article about the accident.

Frank had been right about Shelly's parents being in Switzerland on vacation; the account took up almost a quarter of a page, including a photo of the two. Joda could see the family likeness and remembered telling Egan on that first day that Shelly had looked vaguely familiar.

It had been the Raynalds' custom to travel to the Swiss Alps every year to ski. According to the article, their love of the sport was shared by the elder of their two children, Shelly, but she had been unable to accompany them this time. The couple had been cross-country skiing with six other people and all eight of the skiers had perished by avalanche.

Joda hurried to make copies of the articles and leave the library. Even though she hadn't the least idea how she would use her newly acquired knowledge, it gave her comfort to know that she was much closer to understanding the reason behind Shelly's aberrant actions.

Showered and comfortable in a long housecoat, Joda prepared dinner with her aunt. It was something she hadn't done in a long time. Still, she found everything in exactly the same place it had been for as long as she could remember. Joda appreciated the familiarity of the routine; she cherished the stability of this relationship. If only *all* one's close alliances could be this comfortable.

"Congratulations on the good press, Joda. I guess you're the 'woman of the hour' around town. You used to call and tell me about such things."

"I'm sorry, Aunt Hally, I've been really busy . . . and a little absentminded, too, I suppose." They were both silent for a moment. Joda concentrated on scraping the carrot she had in her hand.

"Are you going to tell me what's going on, or am I going to have to guess?"

"I'm going to tell you. It's just that it's hard to know where to begin."

"You've already told me about Shelly Sloan's accident, and about the lawsuit and about her wanting you fired."

"She *did* file suit and she still wants me fired."

"Well, I don't at all understand what she has against you."

"You're not alone. Nobody else seems to either. But I came up with something today."

Hally's eyes widened. "Tell me," she demanded.

Joda started at the beginning, but she was careful in telling the story; she didn't want her aunt to get too curious about her friendship with Egan O'Neill. She did, however, try to explain how he was involved in the events of the past few weeks.

"So when Egan suggested that you quit your job, you were angry and suspected he'd been lying about giving up the case?"

"Wouldn't you have felt the same way?"

"Perhaps. Go on," Hally insisted.

"Well, the information Frank found out helped me come up with what I discovered today. I'll get to that in just a minute." She started to put the finishing touches on the salad she was preparing. "Now, don't get mad about this. I would have told you sooner, but I didn't want to worry you . . . and some other things came up, and . . ."

Aunt Hally gave her a suspicious look that turned to disbelief as Joda told her about her own accident while skiing Pallavicini run. The disbelief changed back into suspicion, however, as Joda described Egan's visit to Aspenwalk the next day.

"So he still believed that you should quit your job? He's a persistent young fellow. Still, his reasoning is logical. If he really *is* off the case, then I'm hard pressed to find fault with his suggestion that you'd be in a better job-hunting position *before* you're fired rather than after."

Joda carried the salad bowl to the table at one end of the kitchen. "Well, wait until you hear what happened the next day." She turned to watch her aunt pull the steaks out from under the oven broiler and bring them to the table.

"The next day? That would be this past Friday, right?" her aunt asked as Joda transferred the New York strips to the two plates.

"That's right, Friday. Not twenty-four hours after Egan had explained what Shelly might do—she did it!"

"Said she'd drop the suit if Keystone would fire you?"

"Right."

Hally sat down, picked up a bottle of red wine she'd opened earlier and poured both their glasses full. She picked up her glass and held it high for a toast. Joda did the same.

"A toast to Friday," Hally announced wryly, clicked her glass to Joda's, then took a sip. "How in the world did you live through that day, child?" she asked. "The storm, Shelly's change of plans, the rescue of that man—Mr. . . . ah, Forrester. My word, girl, no wonder you haven't had time to call me. How's your steak?"

"Wonderful! A toast to the steak!"

"Hear, hear!"

Joda continued as they ate, bringing Hally up-to-date since Friday, including her strategy used in the television interview. She recounted the story of John Raynald and his parents. She told about everything—except for her painful good-bye to Egan O'Neill.

"I didn't know much about John Raynald, did I?" Hally said thoughtfully when Joda had finished. "Just what you told me and my own impressions when I met him that once. He was a handsome boy, but somehow troubled, I thought. I guess what you've learned today explains the reasons for that."

"And maybe his sister's reasons for the way she's acting, too. It seems a bit unbelievable. I don't know . . . do you think she could have found out that I was the one who taught John to ski and then decided that I was responsible for his death?"

"From everything you've told me, it seems the most logical explanation, Joda. Shelly was hardly in a position to become a mother when she took the job on. It must have been pure agony for her when John started to rebel against her authority; I have a feeling she knew about his feelings for you. And you could hardly expect John to think of Shelly as a real mother figure with real credentials, even though she's obviously been married."

"Maybe she still is."

"Maybe. Maybe not. Anyway, as far as we know for *certain*, John was the only family she had. After losing

her parents to a skiing accident, John's death under
similar circumstances must have practically destroyed
the poor woman. If your theory is true, her belligerence toward you is completely understandable.
Whether knowing her reasons is going to help you or
not remains to be seen, though."

"I have to agree with you. In a way, I hope I'm right.
In a way, I don't. Does that make any sense?"

"Perfect sense." Hally reached over and took
Joda's hand. "First of all, if you're wrong, you'll have
to start all over. Second, if you're right and bring this
all out, Shelly could be dreadfully hurt. I know you
don't want that any more than you want to be hurt
yourself. Also, if she can blame you for John's death,
then there's the possibility that you could start blaming
yourself, even though you know he made his own
choices."

Joda bowed her head. Her aunt was right. She had
already begun to question her own actions. Could she
have done anything that would have prevented John's
crazy race with death? I could have told him that I
loved him! she thought. No, I couldn't have lied to
him.

"You are not responsible, Joda. Not for John's
death and not for Shelly's revenge." She patted her
hand. "Now, let's start thinking ahead. We'll make
some tea and take it in the living room and talk about
the future."

Joda could have easily let depression take over her
mood, but that was not her way.

"I'm going to do nothing," Joda told her aunt when
they were seated in front of the fireplace in the living
room. "I've decided that Keystone will probably delay
any decision to get rid of me as long as I'm riding high
with the local media. I may be wrong about that, but

Mr. Birmingham seemed so frightened when he thought I might refuse to do the television interview."

"From what you told me, I think he may have had second thoughts about what you might have said, too. You really could have given Dennis a scoop, you know?"

Joda smiled and shook her head. "I know," she said quietly.

"I think you're doing the right thing. There are so many ways for something like this to go. Shelly could change her mind. You've only been guessing about what Keystone might do and you could be wrong about that. Doing nothing and keeping your ace in the hole, so to speak, is best."

"Some ace! I'm not sure I'll know how to play it if the time comes that I have to. I don't relish the confrontation." Joda gave a short laugh. "I don't even know for sure if what I hold really *is* an ace. All this speculation about Shelly and her motives could be wrong too, you know?"

"Oh, I know about speculation, all right. I'm the world's champion at it," her aunt said with a sly smile.

"What's that supposed to mean?"

"Not meaning to change the subject—but would you like for me to tell you what I imagine is going on between you and your Egan O'Neill? Just between us speculators?"

"Aunt Hally! There's *nothing* going on between Egan O'Neill and me!"

"You're protesting too much, Joda. Now, sit back and let me tell *you* a story. Feel free to correct me if I'm wrong, okay?"

But there was no need to correct Hally's tale of presumption and misunderstanding, of faith and failure, of provision, and best of all, possibility.

Joda had a good night's sleep for the first time in days and awoke refreshed and ready to return home, take care of Nastar, clean, wash and get ready for the week ahead. She really didn't think her aunt had been right last night when she had said that Egan should not be forgotten, that things were not as they appeared to be, but she'd been so positive, she'd almost gotten Joda to believing their friendship would survive all the trials. Somewhere, deep within her heart, Joda was wishing he would call, explain, make everything right, just like he always had before.

But it didn't happen. The week passed by without a word from anyone about anything. By the next Tuesday morning, Joda felt as if she were sitting on a time bomb just seconds away from detonation.

10

∽∘∞∞∞∞∞∞∞∞∞∞∽

"Nastar! Don't do that!"

Nastar ignored the reprimand and proceeded to continue making paw prints through the ashes that sifted out onto the low brick hearth.

"You do this every time I clean out the fireplace! I should throw you out into the snow!" Joda picked up the heavy gray cat and carried the stubbornly limp body into the kitchen. "You really know how to get attention, don't you?" For some reason, known only to himself, Nastar liked to have his feet wiped off with a damp cloth. "You're a strange cat—yuk!—and a nasty one, too! Look at these feet." Joda had been anxious, frustrated and on edge all week.

There was a knock on the door. "Come in," Joda shouted as she placed Nastar on the kitchen cabinet. "It's not locked."

The sound of the door opening, then: "What would the Board of Health say about *that*, lady?"

It was Egan's voice! Joda looked quickly over her shoulder to find Egan pointing at the furry gray animal on the counter. He was smiling, too. She didn't know

172

whether to be surprised, or angry, or elated, or . . .
She was feeling a little bit of all those things, and more.
He was wearing snug navy corduroy trousers topped
by a gray-and-navy ski sweater that looked Scandinavian, presenting a picture of such vital masculinity and
power that Joda could only stare at him and wonder at
his beauty.

"Am I invited in, or should I back out into the hall
and start all over again?"

"Come in, Egan," she said softly, and turned back
to Nastar.

"May I help?"

Joda allowed him to hold the cat while she wiped
four grimy feet.

"He seems to *like* this."

"He does," Joda said flatly as she finished, then set
the contented cat on the floor.

"You don't seem too happy to see me," Egan said
as Joda straightened. "That's all right," he went on
quickly. "You will be when I tell you my news."

"What news, Egan?" Joda asked warily.

"Kiss me first."

"Egan—" Her words might have stopped him, so
she was glad that the touch of his lips interrupted her.
And it mattered not—for a moment—that they were
traitorous lips. It mattered only that they wanted to kiss
her. How I've missed you, she thought as the familiar
shape of his mouth pressed its warm and precious
outline further into her memory.

But from those same lips had issued her dispposses-
sion. She pulled away. "Egan, why are you here?
Didn't you listen to me?"

His hands at her waist, he held her at arm's length.
"I heard your words—I was *listening* to your heart,
Joda. Come sit with me and you can listen to mine."

All week, despite her good-bye to him, despite the anguish she felt when he had walked away from her, Joda had hoped this would happen, but now she was almost afraid to hear what he had to say. What good could have come of his anger?

"I'm sorry this took so long, Joda, but I had to extricate myself from a very longtime obligation. Shelly and I—"

"Egan," she interrupted him, "you don't have to tell me any of this. In fact, I think I'd rather you wouldn't. Couldn't we just—?"

Egan's finger came up to touch her lips and silence her. "No, Joda, it's not what you're thinking. Shelly's father had always retained the law firm I'm in and when he died I was appointed executor of the estate and trustee of the fund that had been set up for the children. When Shelly had her skiing accident, she naturally came to me for help. I counseled her. From what she told me I thought she had a case, but I wanted to make sure."

"So you came to Keystone as a beginner."

"And I got a different version of how the accident had happened. Not only that, but at the very time I was talking to you, Shelly was deciding on a different course of action. She wanted you fired."

"She called Mr. Birmingham while I was in his office."

"I know. I couldn't believe it. When I found out, we quarreled. I thought I'd persuaded her to forget such a ridiculous idea, but I hadn't." Egan could feel Joda's slight pulling away. "Joda, you *have* to understand." His arm around her shoulder, he drew her closer. "Come here, sweetheart, and listen. I *know* it was hard for you to believe I'd gotten off the case—I don't blame you, after what happened."

"But you predicted it, Egan."

"Without *knowing*, though. As a lawyer, that's my job, to try to figure out the worst that can happen and be ready to counter it. In the courtroom there's nothing worse than being surprised by the opposition. I wanted to protect you as much as I could, but being the family trustee, I was still obligated . . ." He held her even tighter. "That's all over now, Joda, I've resigned as trustee of the Raynald fund, I'm no longer connected with Shelly Sloan in any way. May I tell you why?"

Joda pulled away and turned to look at him. "May I tell you something first?"

"Of course."

"It's just an idea," she began, then proceeded to tell him everything she'd found out about Shelly Sloan and her family and how she herself had inadvertently become involved with them. "I may be wrong, but I believe Shelly blames me for John's death."

"Joda, that's exactly what I came here to tell you."

"But it's not true! I had nothing to do with—"

"I know," he interrupted softly; then: "On the day Shelly learned of John's death, she went into a state of severe depression. Darrel Sloan was a loving and supportive husband through a year of therapy, but when the depression lifted, it was replaced by an obsession for revenge. Shelly could think of nothing else, least of all her husband or her marriage. Darrel couldn't take it anymore. He left her three months ago."

"She blames me for their separation, too."

Egan nodded. "Darrel tried to get her back into therapy, but couldn't; she was beyond reason. She had no real plan. Her broken ankle really was an accident, but it was the perfect one."

"And you learned all this . . . ?"

"This week, when I went to tell her about my resignation. She was so angry she just blurted everything out."

"So you really *have* been on my side all along?"
He nodded.

"Egan, will knowing all of this help me in any way?"
"I'm hoping that—"
Before he could finish, the phone interrupted him. Joda went to answer it. When she returned, Egan looked at her in concern. "What is it, Joda! Is something wrong?"

"That was Mr. Birmingham. Shelly has withdrawn her offer to drop the suit in exchange for my dismissal, and there was something about a medical complication with her broken ankle. The tibia-fibular ligament was torn, they put her in a walking cast without knowing it—it's almost impossible to detect—and the pain brought her right back to the doctor. Now they're saying she can't work and may have to have surgery. She's increased the damages to two million and will settle for Keystone's insurance if they fire me immediately. I don't understand it exactly . . ."

"Well, *I* do!" Egan's temper flared. "She doesn't need the money. She's after only one thing. That does it—I have no choice now." He moved to the phone, and Joda listened as he told the entire story to Shelly's husband and asked for his help.

"Is there any hope?" Joda asked bleakly when Egan had hung up.

"Of course there's hope, Joda!"
But his voice didn't sound as sure as his words.

A full moon lighted their way among the tall pines and aspens of the Arapahoe National Forest, making the night perfect for cross-country skiing. Since Mr. Birmingham's news, neither Egan nor Joda had found it too easy to feel positive about what lay ahead. After Shelly had told Egan the reason behind her vengeful treatment of Joda, she had begged him not to tell her husband what she was doing. She had hopes for a reconciliation, but knew Darrel would never approve of her actions. She was certain, however, that after she had been victorious, Darrel could be convinced that her actions had accomplished nothing but justice and she would deserve his praise instead of his censure. But Egan knew that if Shelly achieved her goal, there wouldn't be the least chance for the marriage to survive. He had betrayed a trust by calling Darrel, but he felt everyone involved would surely suffer if he didn't at least try to give Darrel a chance to talk to her.

Joda and Egan had begun their outing in a state of desolation, but the magic of the night forest began to cast its intoxicating spell. The crisp cold air invigorated the mind and spirit, its stillness a soothing balm as well. A million diamonds sparkled everywhere in the brightness of the moon except in the long black shadows cast by stately timber trees.

Their pace was leisurely for the first half-hour; not a word passed between them as Joda led the way over a well-known trail near her home. The ethereal silence invited contemplation, and Joda couldn't help but think about what seemed to be an inevitable disaster in her life, but being with Egan brought her some peace. That had certainly not always been true.

The Snow Spirit would have smiled at her metaphors. Joda thought of their stormy relationship, a blizzard of conflicting and confounding emotions and opinions. But they had thankfully found their way back to one another through the cold. And now, despite the new adversity, Joda felt as if they had survived the winter. A week ago she wouldn't have dared to dream of spring.

Joda stopped short, turned and motioned for Egan to stop beside her. A finger to her lips asked for silence. In the snow-covered meadow several hundred yards to the north of them a gathering of tawny whitetail deer walked silently across the brightly lit clearing.

"Beautiful," Egan breathed. His shoulder touched hers.

It took only an instant to transmit the message of desire, one to another. A glance, a moment's pause until the graceful animals below had entered the shadows of the forest, then the two silent figures turned toward home.

The fire felt good on cold fingers and toes, a pleasant change from the pristine chill outside, but the beauty of the mountain forest and the strenuous exercise had lifted their spirits somewhat. Joda felt relaxed and comfortable lying next to Egan on the carpet in front of the fire. She snuggled nearer, into the crook of his arm, and felt him tense at the new closeness; then he reached across her, drawing her protectively near.

"I'm so much in love with you, Joda Kerris. I think I've loved you from the very first moment I saw you. Can you ever forgive me for all our misunderstandings?"

"Do you have to ask?"

"Yes."

Joda was almost ashamed to acknowledge her past intolerance, but, "I finally admitted to myself that you were doing what you had to do. I respect that now . . . and I love you all the more for it."

"You can't imagine how much I've wanted to hear you say that. Every day we've been apart has been terrible for me."

"And for me, too. I won't doubt you again, Egan."

He held her tightly then, willing her to feel safe with him and the love he had to give her. But even within the safety of his arms, Joda knew the crisis was coming. Losing her beloved work was going to be as crushing a blow as losing Egan would have been. *How will I survive it?*

Egan distracted her from her dreary thoughts. "This is handy," he said, "a sweater with a zipper." It was slowly being undone.

Joda smiled, thankful for the diversion. "Wait till you see what's underneath. It's not nearly so convenient." She wore a heavy high-necked cotton pullover beneath the wool sweater.

"Now, *that's* resistance!" he said as he pulled the sweater aside. But then his lips were nibbling her ear and whispering, "You know, it doesn't matter what you have on, you're the sexiest woman I've ever seen." One hand was roaming over the soft pink cotton of her shirt, outlining the fullness of her breasts. "See what I mean?" Her nipples were blossoming, their arousal plainly evident even under the densely woven material. His hand crept beneath the shirt, cupping one breast, memorizing its lush contour with sensitive fingertips.

His face was only inches from hers, each line and plane precious to her heart. She lifted a finger to outline the perfection of his lips, then let her hand slide behind his head to guide his mouth to hers. And then he was doing wonderful things to her lips with his tongue and his teeth, tasting and exploring until they were both panting with impatience.

He moved slightly away, and she moaned a quiet plea for his return, but his lips were moving across her stomach, searching for something. They closed over the throbbing bud of her breast and began to draw the taste of their pure love.

Joda could feel a vibrant quivering deep within her, the burning message of her need. She murmured his name, caressing the sound of it with her heart as her hands explored the tense muscles of his back beneath his sweater. She longed to feel his naked body touching hers.

She could stay passive no longer, and when Egan realized that she intended to undress him, he momentarily stopped his assault so she could proceed unhampered. The pleasure of disclosing his body was exquisite to her, every inch of him inviting her appreciative touch. She let her hands tell him how much she loved and wanted him. With shameless directness she explored him. With passion-filled eyes, loving fingers and hungry lips she devoured the beautiful secrets of his desire for her.

"You're driving me insane!" he rasped breathlessly. And with the agility of a dancer he had lifted her away and lowered her to her back on the carpet. "My turn," he breathed, as he grasped the bottom of her shirt.

"That's not fair," she protested as he lifted her arms and slipped the cotton shirt off over her head, holding her wrists captive while his tongue explored the rosy peak of her breast.

"You can tell me to stop whenever you like," he teased, but there was no taunting in his eyes, only appreciation for the woman below him. He released her wrists then and deftly divested her of the remainder of her clothing, sliding his hands back up her long legs, touching, kissing, discovering her as she had done to him only moments before.

A searing heat flared through her body and she curled forward, grasping his shoulders, digging her fingers into his flesh. "Please, Egan!" she gasped. "Please."

"Like this?" he asked, easing his weight forward and over her trembling body.

"Yes . . . Egan, yes," she breathed as he accepted her invitation.

He entered her slowly, savoring the union, revering the completeness they possessed. The rhythm of passion seized them and dictated their unison and Joda knew with certainty that she would always belong to this man, no matter what her future held.

"You own me, sweetheart," he whispered as they lay exhausted in each other's arms. "I never want to be separated from you again. Marry me, Joda."

She held him tightly, as if he might get away if she were to loosen her hold. She felt the same way, but with one reservation. Without her work she knew she would not be the same person he was in love with right now.

"I can't marry you, Egan."

He leaned abruptly away from her and looked into her eyes. "What are you saying?"

"Without my work I'm going to be miserable and mean, Egan. *Please* try to understand . . . you'll hate me. I know it."

"Impossible! I forbid you to even think such a thing!"

"I don't think it . . . I know it."

"No one can know the future."

"But I know myself. Please . . . let's just not talk

about it anymore," she said miserably, tears forming in her eyes. "Please, Egan, just know that I love you and let that be enough."

"Never!"

But within twenty-four hours after Egan's abrupt departure, Joda was called into Mr. Birmingham's office and given the two weeks notice her contract called for. Self-pity followed her home where only Nastar waited. Joda could barely see him through her tears. The fireplace remained black and cold, no lights were turned on to brighten the gloom of evening.

A painful knot coiled tightly in Joda's stomach and she thought she was going to die with the misery of it as she sat cross-legged on the bed and stared across the room. She could neither eat, nor sleep, nor think of the future in any way except through grief. Self-pity filled her world, and there was room for nothing else. Egan did not exist.

Through the long night Joda found no peace in the lonely darkness or in the prison of her mind. The phone rang, but it was left unanswered. Finally, at dawn, she undressed, only to dress again after a quick shower. She despaired at having to go to work; there was no joy left in teaching, no joy left anywhere in her world.

Joda's instructors for the handicapped classes were already busy with their individual charges when she arrived, and she found a spunky Janice waiting eagerly for her day on the mountain.

"You look mad," the thirteen-year-old said as Joda guided her foot into the binding on one of her specially designed skis.

"I'm not!" Joda snapped.

"Okay! Okay! Pardon me all to heck!"

Janice's rebuke sparked a feeling of remorse. "I'm sorry," she said stiffly. "If I'm angry, it's not at you." She tousled the girl's short hair. "You ready? Let's go."

Janice's moderate cerebral palsy made skiing difficult to say the least, but as usual, her iron will and self-discipline guided her down the slopes again and again. Over the weeks, Joda had brought Janice through a living hell, from total aversion to unfaltering resolution of purpose. Muscles toned, stamina increased, determined, Janice attacked the mountain with the persistence of the winter wind.

"Get up!" Joda shouted as she slid to a stop beside Janice's sprawling body.

"Gimme a minute!"

"You've been lying there so long, you're going to forget how to ski by the time you get up." Joda had found that a benevolent strictness achieved the best results with Janice.

But sometimes Janice rebelled against it. "Go on, then, leave me here. See if I care!"

"Are you getting lazy on me?"

"No! I'm just tired of your pouting!"

Joda was shocked. Since that first harsh word this morning, she was sure she'd effectively masked her unhappiness from the child. Maybe it was something else. She knelt beside the girl. "Janice, did you hurt yourself?" she asked gently, knowing that Janice was reluctant ever to admit a setback of any kind.

"No!" she answered too quickly; then, reluctantly: "Maybe. It's nothing!" she added hastily. She was rubbing her leg above her ski boot.

"Let me check." Joda loosened the boot and began to feel along Janice's leg and ankle. Nothing was broken, thank goodness, but the ankle was a tricky thing. Joda didn't want to take any chances, and under protest, Janice waited while Joda called for the ski patrol and a sled.

A young boy, his arm in a sling, sat on a stretcher next to Janice's as Dr. White examined her ankle. His nine-year-old curiosity and candidness compelled him to ask, "How can you ski like that?"

Janice was a veteran at fielding such heartless questions. "It's easy. I wear the skis on my head."

"Come on, get serious." He hopped off the stretcher.

"Tommy, why don't you wait out front?" Dr. White gave Joda an apologetic look.

"It's okay, Doc," Janice said. "Let him stay. He might learn something."

"Can you really ski?" Tommy asked.

"Sure."

"I don't believe you."

"You think I'd be up here in the freezing cold if I couldn't?"

Tommy gave her a long, studied look. "Why do you do it?"

"'Cause if I can lick that mountain out there, I can lick anything." She smiled up at Joda, and Joda recognized her own words.

"Oh. I get it," Tommy said knowingly; then he walked out of the room.

"I think he really *did* learn something," Janice said casually.

The doctor and Joda exchanged looks; he winked, she beamed.

"This kid's okay," Dr. White said to Joda, as if unaffected by the moving scene they'd just witnessed.

"You mean I have to go back out there and ski some

more?" Joda teased. "I was hoping to take the rest of the day off!"

"Let's get out of here, Teach."

"In just a minute," Joda said. "May I make a phone call first?"

I've just learned something, too, and now I have a mountain of my own to conquer.

"If you have to!"

"I have to!"

From Dr. White's office Joda placed her call and charged it to her home phone.

"Hello."

"Will you marry me?"

"Who is this?" Egan asked playfully.

"The Snow Spirit."

"Do I know you?"

"Better than I know myself."

"I'll testify to that . . . and I accept."

"The jury's out right now. Would you testify again tonight?"

"Will there be any witnesses?"

"None."

"I'll be there."

"Bring champagne."

"You've got it."

"Champagne?" Mr. Birmingham said loudly as he walked into the doctor's office. "Joda, how did you know you had something to celebrate?"

"I'm engaged, Mr. Birmingham." Her smile was radiant.

"Now, that's worth celebrating!"

"I know." Joda walked past him to the door.

"Hey, wait a minute. Don't you want to hear my good news?"

"Oh . . . sure." Her mind was preoccupied with

Janice's lesson and the victory over her own debilitating self-pity.

"You're also re-engaged."

"I . . . don't know what that means, Mr. B."

"The lawsuit has been dropped."

Joda's eyes widened in disbelief. "Shelly's lawsuit?"

"That's right. Frank said to tell you 'Darrel worked a miracle.'" He shrugged. "Frank didn't seem to understand it either."

Joda grabbed him, kissed his cheek, then held him in a bear hug. "Mr. B., I love you!"

"Hey, there! I thought you were an engaged woman!"

"And re-engaged, too!" She released him. "Thank you, boss." She went back to Janice. "Okay, kid." She rubbed her hands together. "Hit the slopes. Your lazy days are over. No more lounging around for you today."

"Hey, you're not pouting anymore!"

"I will be if you don't get yourself in gear!"

"Slave driver!"

"Renegade!"

"Tyrant!"

Joda hugged the girl to her side as she helped her off the stretcher, then kissed the top of her head. "Tiger."

Joda turned her key in the lock and opened the front door, expecting Nastar's usual trill in greeting. Her mouth fell open in surprise. The living room had been transformed. It looked like a New Year's Eve party. Gaily colored balloons hung everywhere and a huge bouquet of fresh flowers stood on the dining table beside at least a dozen bottles of champagne. On the small square table beside the couch, a brand-new pair of Tant Mieux ski boots gleamed bright red.

Joda couldn't believe what she was seeing and stood fixed to the spot in the doorway. Her eyes went to the couch. Along its complete length, propped against the back cushions, was a line of pictures, all of them done in needlepoint. She moved toward them, knelt down, and stared. Each one was original, as different from the next as faces in a crowd . . . but each one was entitled *Snow Spirit.*

"A wedding gift. From the kids."

Joda whirled around at the sound of Egan's voice. He had been quietly standing in a corner of the kitchen all the time. She glanced at the pictures again, then back at the man who was walking toward her.

"Egan, how did they know?" she asked as she stood up.

"I told them," he answered simply.

"But . . . it takes a long time to . . ."

"About a month." His hands were on her waist.

Joda glared at him. "Egan, I just proposed to you this morning. Can you explain how you knew what . . . ?"

"Intuition."

"Egan . . ."

"The Snow Spirit told me," he said innocently, "a long time ago."

Joda smiled. "Me, too."

Silhouette Desire
15-Day Trial Offer
A new romance series that explores contemporary relationships in exciting detail

Six Silhouette Desire romances, free for 15 days!
We'll send you six new Silhouette Desire romances
to look over for 15 days, absolutely free! If you decide
not to keep the books, return them and owe nothing.

Six books a month, free home delivery. If you like
Silhouette Desire romances as much as we think you
will, keep them and return your payment with the
invoice. Then we will send you six new books every
month to preview, just as soon as they are published.
You pay only for the books you decide to keep, and
you never pay postage and handling.

Silhouette Desire

Coming Next Month

Price of Surrender by Stephanie James

Holt Sinclair thought everything had its price until he met a woman who couldn't be bought. Adena West had come to him on business but Holt was more interested in pleasure. She entered his corporate jungle to become passion's prey.

Sweet Serenity by Billie Douglass

When Serena was a child, Tom Reynolds destroyed her happy life. With Tom's reappearance all the old hurt returned. Although he made her tremble with passion, Serena vowed not to fall beneath his spell.

Gentle Conquest by Kathryn Mallory

When rock star Stuart North agreed to buy and preserve historic Brogan House, he wanted gray-eyed Robin Elliot as part of the deal. What he didn't bargain for was the electricity between them that burst into a flashfire of passion.

Silhouette Desire

Coming Next Month

Seduction by Design by Erin St. Claire

From the very beginning Tyler Scott made his intentions clear to Hailey — he intended to be her lover. He radiated a raw masculine power that left Hailey helpless with desire and unable to resist him.

Shadow of Betrayal by Nicole Monet

Diana Moreland tried to hate Joshua Cambridge especially now that he returned to claim his son; the nephew she raised all alone. Desperately she fought to keep the child and her heart — and lost both.

Ask Me No Secrets by Ruth Stewart

The past was behind her, and when Allison looked into Forrest Bennett's coal-black eyes she knew the future held a glowing promise of love. But would he love her still when he penetrated to the secret heart of her passion?

YOU'LL BE SWEPT AWAY
WITH SILHOUETTE DESIRE

$1.75 each

1 ☐ CORPORATE AFFAIR
James

2 ☐ LOVE'S SILVER WEB
Monet

3 ☐ WISE FOLLY
Clay

4 ☐ KISS AND TELL Carey

5 ☐ WHEN LAST WE LOVED
Baker

6 ☐ A FRENCHMAN'S KISS
Mallory

7 ☐ NOT EVEN FOR LOVE
Claire

8 ☐ MAKE NO PROMISES
Dee

9 ☐ MOMENT IN TIME
Simms

10 ☐ WHENEVER I LOVE YOU
Smith

$1.95 each

11 ☐ VELVET TOUCH
James

12 ☐ THE COWBOY AND THE
LADY Palmer

13 ☐ COME BACK, MY LOVE
Wallace

14 ☐ BLANKET OF STARS
Valley.

15 ☐ SWEET BONDAGE
Vernon

16 ☐ DREAM COME TRUE
Major

17 ☐ OF PASSION BORN
Simms

18 ☐ SECOND HARVEST
Ross

19 ☐ LOVER IN PURSUIT
James

20 ☐ KING OF DIAMONDS
Allison

21 ☐ LOVE IN THE CHINA SEA
Baker

22 ☐ BITTERSWEET IN BERN
Durant

23 ☐ CONSTANT STRANGER
Sunshine

24 ☐ SHARED MOMENTS
Baxter

25 ☐ RENAISSANCE MAN
James

26 ☐ SEPTEMBER MORNING
Palmer

27 ☐ ON WINGS OF NIGHT
Conrad

28 ☐ PASSIONATE JOURNEY
Lovan

29 ☐ ENCHANTED DESERT
Michelle

30 ☐ PAST FORGETTING
Lind

31 ☐ RECKLESS PASSION
James

32 ☐ YESTERDAY'S DREAMS
Clay

33 ☐ PROMISE ME
TOMORROW Powers

34 ☐ SNOW SPIRIT
Milan

35 ☐ MEANT TO BE
Major

36 ☐ FIRES OF MEMORY
Summers

Silhouette Desire

Now Available

Reckless Passion by Stephanie James

Dana Bancroft's stockbroker sense told
her that beneath Yale Ransom's well groomed exterior
there lurked a primal force . . . anxiously
waiting to be released.

Yesterday's Dreams by Rita Clay

He said his name was "Mr. Lawrence," but
Candra Bishop soon discovered the truth: he was the
stable boy she had adored in her youth.

Promise Me Tomorrow by Nora Powers

Harris Linton was a charmer, the kind of
man artist Jessie Hampton despised—yet couldn't
resist. She knew she couldn't trust him but desire
overpowered rational thought.

Snow Spirit by Angel Milan

Joda Kerris' passions flared when she discovered that
Egan, the man she had fallen in love with, was a lawyer
hired to sue her and Keystone Mountain Ski Resort!

Meant To Be by Ann Major

Before she knew he was her boss, ravishing
Leslie Grant abandoned herself to Boone Dexter for a
single passionate night. How could she convince
him she loved him?

Fires Of Memory by Ashley Summers

Just when Gia Flynn thought he was safely out
of her life, Adam Kendricks, real-estate tycoon,
returned to San Francisco. This time she would
conquer him once and for all.